Caught in the Current

Caught in the Current

A Cape Cod Shore Romance

Charlee James

TULE

Caught in the Current
Copyright © 2018 Charlee James
Tule Publishing First Printing, August 2018

The Tule Publishing Group, LLC

ALL RIGHTS RESERVED

First Publication by Tule Publishing Group 2018

No part of this book may be used or reproduced in any manner whatsoever without written permission except in the case of brief quotations embodied in critical articles and reviews.

This is a work of fiction. Names, characters, places, and incidents are products of the author's imagination or are used fictitiously. Any resemblance to actual events, locales, organizations, or persons, living or dead, is entirely coincidental.

ISBN: 978-1-949068-98-6

For Laura with love, and to sisters everywhere.

Chapter One

Biting February winds howled over the dark, tossing waves and snaked down the neck of Jason Hall's sweatshirt. The dicey surf mirrored the sickening churn in his gut. It had been seventy-two hours since his nephew Luke was taken. Seventy-two hours since Jason had last slept. He'd scoured every inch of the seaside town his family called home for the teenager who always had a lacrosse stick or baseball glove in hand. Amber Alerts flashed Luke's picture, one from his last middle school dance.

It seemed like yesterday that Jay had pulled up to the school, crowded with nervous teens, as they waited to get into the gym for the dance. They'd talked and laughed on the ride, and he'd given Luke advice on the best way to ask Shae Brigham to slow dance. Now, Luke's freckled face flew across television screens throughout the region, but the hours ticked by with no new information.

Jay was done sitting on the sidelines while his baby sister cried jagged tears. Done seeing the helpless devastation in his aging parents' eyes. He drew in the salt-laced air. It did nothing to cool the burn in the back of his throat. It was up to him to find Luke now.

A low bark made him glance over his shoulder. He'd called on all his resources to help in the search. Fellow veterans and brothers-in-arms were on the hunt, but the badass private investigator taking purposeful, no-nonsense strides across the beach was his greatest hope of finding Luke. A beast of a dog walked dutifully at her hip. Dark clothing clung to her slim frame, accentuating every subtle curve, and a weapon was holstered at her hip.

He patted the solid Beretta concealed under his shirt and relaxed his shoulders, forcing the stiffness there to subside. Alex Macintyre was petite but she carried herself with power. The first and last time he'd seen her they'd been steaming up the windows of her black SUV after they met by chance over dinner with mutual friends.

Fiery red hair slapped against her jawline as the impending storm rolled to a boil overhead.

"Talk to me," Alex said when she was within arm's length. They began walking down the shoreline together, hip to hip.

"My nephew's thirteen. He was taken by his biological father on Friday during an unauthorized visit at my sister's house." Jay pulled out his wallet and handed over a picture of Luke, elbow deep in a banana split.

"And now it's Sunday evening, and nothing?" She glanced at him and he caught a flash of her bourbon-colored eyes.

"It's like they disappeared without a trace."

Alex stopped and stood solidly next to him. "There's always a trace."

A coil of tension between his shoulder blades released, easing the ache there. "And that's exactly why I called you. I'm not asking you to break the law, but I have a hunch you can pass by some of the red tape holding up the investigation."

"Tell me more about the father." Alex kicked a clump of seaweed out of her way as they continued their walk down the beach.

"Lowlife." Jay grunted. "Just got out of jail for assault and battery. He's been in and out of prison Luke's entire life. He did some stints for dealing in front of a playground, breaking and entering, that sort of thing."

"Sounds like a nice guy." Sarcasm dripped from her husky voice. "How'd your sister get tangled up with someone like that?"

"Amy started dating Shane in high school. I'll never forget the day he drove up to our house on his piece of junk motorbike, tracked mud over my mother's clean floors and insulted the sergeant, then left behind the smell of cigarettes and weed when he and Amy walked out the front door." Jay shook his head. The guy was a punk then, just as he was now.

"So, military service runs in the family, then?" Alex put a steady hand on the dog's head as a group of seagulls launched into the air ahead of them.

"Dad had a long career as an E-7 gunnery sergeant. He forbade Amy from seeing this guy, but she went behind his back, and when she got pregnant, Shane dropped out of school."

He let out a sigh. His parents had approved of *his* high school sweetheart—a bit too much. They were disappointed when he broke it off after his discharge, and he never could bring himself to tell them what she'd done. It was a small town where gossip flew around faster than a fighter jet. She'd wronged him, but he was man enough not to bad-mouth an ex.

"I'm guessing that wasn't to play the role of doting father." The side-eye she shot him made his blood pump faster. Alex was a looker.

"Yeah, he bolted. The pregnancy changed Amy, though. She started being diligent about schoolwork and took good care of herself. When Luke was born, Amy doted on him. She never took advantage of us living under one roof. If she wanted help she had it, but Amy rarely asked." Jay followed Alex's lead and stopped a few feet before a jetty. Foam formed around the jagged rocks from the battering water below.

"I'd like to ask her some questions. I know the police have gone over it a thousand times, but I need my own perspective." Thunder rattled the air around them. Alex didn't flinch but the dog trembled behind her. Her wide stance mirrored his as they paused for a moment.

"I get it. When can we start the search?" Heat coursed through his body like a flash fire devouring trees and dried brush. He wanted to find that son of a bitch who took Luke and wronged his sister. And if Jay didn't find his nephew alive and well, Shane would be on his knees praying for the end.

"Now," Alex said. Lightning electrified the sky, illuminating the hard glint in her eyes. Yes, there was no doubt he'd made the right decision to call her. Like the storm that exploded above them, she was a force to be reckoned with.

So was he.

Chapter Two

A LEX SAT ON the edge of the love seat with her feet firmly planted on the ground next to Hank and her hands steepled together on her lap. Jay and his sister sat across from her on the faded blue couch in the modest, two-story Cape Cod house. Family photos were meticulously lined on the wall and knickknacks stood straight as soldiers on the mantels and shelves. Amy let out a wrenching sob and used the palms of both hands to wipe away her tears. Jay's Adam's apple bobbed and the corded muscle of his arm flexed as he draped it over his sister's shoulders.

"Did you ever talk to Luke about his father?" Alex didn't need a notebook to record the responses. Most of the answers she needed wouldn't be verbalized.

"I don't like to talk about that part of my life." Amy's eyes darted toward the door with two dead bolts. "I didn't want Luke to resent me."

"How so?" Alex asked, tempering her tone so it was softer.

"I knew Shane wasn't the settle-down type but I didn't care. I cost Luke a stable father because I was so…careless."

Amy twisted the chain at her neck.

"He was responsible for his own actions, just like he is now." Jay hugged his sister a bit tighter and hunched over to kiss the top of her head.

"Did you have any contact with Shane after you broke up?"

Amy picked at her cuticles and shook her head no. "Can I get either of you something to drink?"

Jay started to say no, but Alex jumped in. "A water would be great. Thanks." Amy scurried off to the kitchen and Alex met Jay's eyes.

"For the sake of saving time, why don't you go up to Luke's room? See if there's anything there that might tell us something. I'll meet you up there. Another picture or two wouldn't hurt either," Alex said. Jay's eyes narrowed but he pushed off the couch.

"Go easy on her. She seems so…fragile." Jay's words were a low, gritty whisper. Alex couldn't help but steal a glance at his toned backside and broad shoulders as he took the stairs to the second floor two at a time. She'd had her hands on his taut stomach and chest one hot August evening, but they'd never finished what they started.

"Here." Amy returned with a glass. Alex took it from her and noticed a slight tremor as Amy moved her hand away. "I'm so sorry. I ran out of bottled. I should've gone to the store."

"Water's water," Alex answered, and drank deeply before

setting the glass on the coffee table. "How did you and Shane meet?"

"I'm sorry, but I don't see how my past is going to help find Luke," Amy said weakly.

Alex stood up and skirted around the table, choosing to sit next to Jay's sister, rather than across from her. The dog followed her lead and chose to sit next to Amy. This was Hank's specialty, lending comfort to the emotionally fragile. For a mastiff he was a big wimp, but what he lacked in bravado he made up for in his quiet ability to soothe.

"Your past with Shane can tell us a lot. Maybe even give us clues where they might be headed, why he took him, what kind of treatment Luke is receiving." Alex let the last statement hang and waited for a response.

"He was never really violent with me, if that's what you're insinuating." Amy looked down at the floor then met her eyes.

"Really violent? Amy, if he did something to you, it wasn't your fault. Even the littlest detail might help." Alex kept her distance and waited.

"It was, though. There was one night we went to a party. I actually stuffed an outfit in my purse because I knew my father would never let me out of the house with it on." A blank expression crossed Amy's face.

"And what happened at the party, Amy?" Alex said softly. Hank placed his head on Amy's leg, and she placed a hand on his head.

"I started it. Kissing him, touching him. I had never planned to actually, you know, go any further."

Alex heard footsteps on the floor upstairs. She just needed a few more minutes. "But it did go further," she said.

"It wasn't fair to stop after I'd turned him on. I shouldn't have resisted." Amy wrapped her arms around her waist and leaned forward. "But I did. He put a pillow over my face. I couldn't breathe. That's all I remember. We were drunk. I guess we were both at fault." Tears clouded her eyes. "Then, I missed my period. When I told him, he was angry. He did slap me then."

"Did you tell anyone?" She pulled a tissue from the box on the table in front of them and handed it to Amy. She wiped her eyes and blew her nose.

"Until Luke disappeared, I couldn't recall what happened clearly. It just all came flooding back." Her voice cracked on the last word.

"None of this was your fault." She got up and crossed the room, dug a card out of her bag, and returned to the couch. She held out the thick cardstock and squatted on the floor next to Amy. "That's the contact information for my friend, Julia Jones. She's a specialist at a rape crisis center. I have an open invitation to share that she's a survivor, too."

"It's just that it has been so long since it all happened…" Amy grabbed up another tissue from the box. Mascara was smudged under her eyes, adding to the dark circles that also rested there.

"The Massachusetts Statute of Limitations gives victims fifteen years to come forward. You can still take legal action against him. I understand it's a difficult decision. One that Julia can help you navigate." The stairs creaked and Alex glanced toward Jay, who was carrying something in his hand.

"What's going on?" Jay started toward Amy but she held her hands up and stepped back.

"I don't want to talk anymore. Alex can fill you in if she wants, but I need to go lie down." Amy started to retreat toward the stairs.

"Is there someone you'd like me to call? Someone who can stay with you for a bit?" Alex ignored the hard lines that had formed on Jay's face.

"Jay," Amy said, looking past Alex. "Can you have Sis come over?"

"Of course." Jay searched Amy's face. "Best little sis." The simple words of endearment gripped at her heart.

"Best big bro," Amy whispered. Alex looked away and ignored the pain in her ribs. She'd never have that sibling bond; it had been snatched away the day her sister was lured into the back seat of a white van.

"I had a feeling you were trying to get rid of me in there," Jay said in a deep tone once they were in the driveway. He paced around the hood of her SUV and swung open the back door for Hank before sliding into the front beside her.

"I just had this feeling. It turned out to be correct." Alex wished her hunch hadn't been right. She clutched the steering wheel a little tighter as they drove.

"Tell me," Jay said through a clenched jaw.

Alex hesitated for a moment. "Shane raped her," she said gently.

"What…what did you just say?" His warm amber eyes chilled to flinty stone.

"She didn't recall what had happened until now. Luke's disappearance triggered the memory of the assault." She took a deep breath and looked over at his rigid frame.

"Pull over." His voice was hoarse and menacing.

Alex put on her directional and turned onto a dirt road. The vehicle bumped over the unpaved surface until she hit the brakes and parked. Jay lifted a hand over his mouth, then after a second shoved open the door. He stood away from the SUV, rod straight, and looked out at an army of trees. She gave him a few moments, then joined him. The scent of fresh pine tickled her nose as she walked down and stood at his side.

"I should have protected her. How the hell didn't I see it?" His nostrils flared, and the jagged scar that was split over the right side of his face seemed to intensify.

"You shouldn't take the blame." It was hard to choke out the words. It was almost hard not to laugh at the irony of them.

"I failed her." Jay spat out the words and sent his fist flying into a nearby tree. His hand connected with a thud and bark shattered into the air. When blood ran down his knuckles he didn't seem to notice. Heat spread over her back like a sunburn after a long beach day, and her cheeks went numb. She wouldn't have a panic attack now, when Jay and his nephew needed her. The scenario they were dealing with just hit too close to home. She closed her eyes and took a few counted breaths. In through the nose, out through the mouth. Alex forced her muscles to relax starting with her shoulders and working her way down until she had mellowed out.

"You'll get your chance at revenge, but right now your family needs you. Luke needs you. Don't let your judgment get sloppy."

"I nearly forgot." Jay reached into his back pocket and pulled out a handful of envelopes. "He must've gotten curious about his father, or the other way around, but I found letters from Shane under Luke's bed. I only read the first one before I heard Amy crying."

"It's normal to be curious about a biological parent. It makes me wonder if he went with Shane of his own free will." Had Amy known anything about this?

"Luke wouldn't have realized the danger in having a face-to-face, because he never was told anything about his father." A line formed between Jay's brows. "I understand why, but it might be a factor."

"This gives us a starting point. Come back to the inn with me. We'll read the rest of the letters and determine our next steps." Alex wanted to get this investigation started immediately. Not because she'd left the entire staff of her PI firm working extra hours to fill in the gaps she was leaving open, but because they were eclipsing the seventy-five-hour mark. Every moment counted.

Chapter Three

THE SEA HORSE Inn tended to do a decent business in the slow season, filling up with associations and corporate retreats. Good for the local economy. Not good when you were in a rush to park. After Alex circled the lot a few times strain balled up in Jay's chest, then she whipped the wheel right and stole a spot from a Mercedes. The other driver smacked his hands against the posh steering wheel, started to flip her the bird, but cringed back when Jay shot him a death stare. It was the same reaction most had to the deep scars on Jay's face. He didn't give a shit. He'd earned these scars enduring the searing pain of shrapnel.

Alex nodded in approval as the driver averted his eyes and drove past them. Simultaneously, they opened the car doors, and Alex leashed Hank. The arctic air numbed his exposed hands and face. He glanced at Alex. Her thin zip-up hoodie would do little to block the chill. He grasped one of the sea-horse-shaped handles, opened the door to the main lobby, and was grateful for the heat pumping through the vents.

Alex gave the girl at the front desk a brisk wave and

strode right to the elevator. She pushed the button to go up, while he tapped his fingers impatiently against the sand-dollar-papered wall. When they got to the second floor, they walked briskly along the peach-colored carpet embossed with shells until they stopped in front of Alex's room.

"Home sweet home," Alex murmured. She slid her key card into the lock and pushed it open. The giant dog pushed past them both and filled up the small entryway, then sat on the carpet with a long string of drool hanging off his jowls, his tail ticking back and forth expectantly. A grin spread over Alex's face, and she squatted down to rub both hands over the dog's face and neck. "I was lucky to find a place that allows dogs." She gave him a kiss on the head. "All right, back up, boy. We have work."

Jay paused to pat the friendly monster's head. Alex squeezed past, her body unintentionally brushing up against his. The entryway was too cramped for a big man and a big dog. He followed her into a guest room big enough for a queen-sized bed, a small sofa, and a desk and chair. On the corner of the bed were a few dog toys including a floppy blue bunny. Jay nearly grinned. You could learn a lot about a person by how they treated an animal.

"Come on, Hank." Alex slapped one hand against her hip and the dog bounded toward her, put its massive paws on her shoulders, and lapped his tongue over her face before hopping up on the bed. A grin was still stretched across Alex's lips when she dropped into the desk chair. He lowered onto the peach-colored love seat across from her. The room suddenly seemed very small. Alex leaned forward, resting her forearms against her legs.

"Okay, let's see what lies Shane was spinning to Luke." Alex extended her hand.

"There're a lot of letters. We'll each take half." His fingers brushed the stiff papers folded inside his pocket and he pulled them out. Without counting, he split the pile in two and was already reading as he held the rest out to Alex. They sat in silence, the only sound the rustle of papers and Hank's tail occasionally slapping against the sea-inspired bedding.

Alex sucked in a breath, and his eyes shot up from the paragraph where Shane was telling Luke how hard he tried to be part of his life. All his muscles corded with tension, and his skin crawled from the lies written to deceive a child.

"Right here." Alex tapped the page. "He's telling Luke he has a bungalow by the ocean in Florida." She cleared her throat and read. "*It would be so cool to teach you how to surf. Then we could hang on the beach and watch all the babes in their bikinis—I might even let you have a beer or two. I've called your mom a few times but she wants you all to herself. It's not fair. I really want to be part of your life, man.*" A long breath whistled through Alex's teeth. Her eyes lowered to Jay's hands and back up to his face. "Ease up before you destroy the evidence."

Jay glanced down to where his hands crushed the papers into a ball. He loosened his grip, and his red fingers began to fade back to a normal color.

"I can't believe this guy. He's making it seem like the sergeant and my mom were so judgmental about his motorcycle and a few piercings that they drove him away from Amy when she discovered she was pregnant. That he'd tried to stay and provide for them. Even goes into how he bought Amy a ring and asked my father for her hand so they could be a family." There was a tremor in his voice.

"Just enough truth mixed into the lies to make a thirteen-year-old believe. If your father is as rigid as you've let on, Luke's probably experienced that, especially as he gets older. He'd believe what Shane is telling him." Her slim fingers swept through her hair.

"I wouldn't say rigid—disciplined, maybe. We needed the structure." He loved his father. Respected him. He didn't want his name used to mislead and lure his nephew away.

"I get it. Nothing about this is going to be easy." Alex stared at him for a moment or two before looking back down at the papers.

They continued reading wordlessly to the song of humming heat flowing through the vent and Hank's jarring snore. A lot of the letters contained chitchat in response to what must have been in Luke's original correspondence—favorite video games, the latest rock band he was listening to, and comments on his school life. Every paragraph or so, Shane subtly put Amy down. Mentioning how awesome Luke was to put up with a mom who just didn't "get it." He smoothed the next letter against his jeans, and as he began reading his pulse kicked up a notch. He scanned through it quickly until he found what they were looking for.

"That son of a bitch," Jay growled and held out the thin piece of paper to Alex. "Fourth paragraph, second line."

After a moment Alex looked up. "That's pretty ballsy, arranging to meet Luke on his home turf while Amy was at work. So, Luke agreed to the setup, but nothing was said about leaving the Cape together."

"I want to know where Shane got his hands on a 'hot classic Camaro.' Maybe he offered to take Luke for a joy ride, never intending to bring him back." What was Shane's endgame? To hurt Amy, his family—or something more sinister?

Alex picked up her cell and made a call while glancing over the remainder of the letter.

"Gabe, I need you to run a search. First- and second-generation Camaros stolen between February fifth and tenth. I think they started manufacturing those in 1967. Call me back." She put the phone back on the desk. "What?" she said when she locked eyes with him.

"I'm insanely impressed by your car knowledge." For the first time in days he smiled.

"My dad was into the classics. He had a 1968 Shelby and loved to show it off. He'd take it, and us, to shows, mainly to give my mom a break." She frowned. Maybe it wasn't a happy memory for her.

"Who's us?" Late-afternoon sunlight streaming through the white gauzy curtains illuminated Alex's hair in a crown of reds and golds.

"My sister, Stephanie." Alex stood up and the chair rolled back. Hank instantly jumped up and was at her heels as she walked to the bathroom. Alex was back in an instant. It seemed everything she did was carried out with a brisk efficiency. She sat back on the chair and rolled toward him so her knees were lightly pressed against his inner thighs.

"Let's see that hand, Rocky," Alex said as she liberally doused a face cloth in rubbing alcohol. He glanced down at his hand, was surprised to see blood caked there, and held it out to Alex.

She grasped it firmly and pressed the cloth against the wound. He gritted his teeth. The stinging sensation wasn't pleasant but her smooth skin against his was. "Ease up there, Nurse Ratched," he said when his gut did an uncomfortable flip-flop. A casual hookup on occasion was fine in his book, but the tender feeling that threatened to creep in as she looked after his hand was not.

"There." Alex wrapped a layer of gauze over his knuckles and secured it with tape. "Now I won't have to pay a damage fee when you drip blood on the carpet." She went to return the supplies to where they came from.

"What's it like living with Dr. Kevorkian?" he asked Hank, who scooted closer to him in response. The dog dropped its head on his leg and Jay stroked his bandaged hand down the bullmastiff's sleek, fawn-colored coat. When Alex came back, Hank could hardly contain his wiggle of excitement. Jay chuckled. "She was just in the bathroom, dude. Not outer space."

"Doesn't take much to delight Hank." She kissed him on the nose. "Best man I've ever met."

Alex's phone chimed and she swiveled to answer. "Hey, Gabe. Find anything?" Her eyes, the color of a tumbler of Johnnie Walker, were intensely focused. She nodded her head and grunted at something that was said. "Thanks, Gabe. Send me a text when you wrap up the fraud case." She hung up the phone and their eyes met.

Everything about her knocked him back like a well-planted roundhouse kick. He wasn't immune to Alex. Their first and last kiss had sizzled like intense August heat and left him unsteady. If it hadn't, they would've finished what they'd started. No, it definitely wasn't a physical relationship with Alex that he feared. Love had kicked him in the ass once. He'd never forgive Becky for what she'd done, and he wouldn't blindly fall into another relationship. Becky had been his high school sweetheart, and they had a long history, most of which was happy. Yet she'd betrayed him in the worst way. Yup, he was all set in the relationship department.

"A 1970 Chevy Camaro was reported as stolen in Foxboro on February seventh. That's the day after Shane was released and only a hop, skip, and jump from the prison where he was serving time." Alex twisted the top off one of the hotel's water bottles, took a long drink. She extended one to him and he took it. Tingles spread across his fingertips as skin brushed against skin during the exchange.

He broke eye contact and picked up the conversation. "The letter that mentions the car is postmarked a week before that. What are the odds you'd be able to find the exact car you're looking for in the exact place you need it?"

"My thoughts exactly." Alex rose from the chair in one fluid movement, flipped her hair back, and placed a hand on the butt of her weapon. "I'm sure the owner of the car will be able to tell us a thing or two."

He nodded. "And after that?" Jay knew exactly what he'd be doing, but he needed to see if Alex was on the same page. He'd pay her whatever she asked to find his nephew.

"If we're lucky enough to get information on where Shane is going, I'll follow the trail and keep you updated from the road." Alex turned her back to him and started filling up a duffel bag. "I'll throw this in my car, so no time is wasted."

"I need to stop by Veterans' Services. Get a few things from my office and make sure there's coverage." The moment he spoke the words Alex's body tensed, and he waited, sure she was going to protest.

"Jay, you don't need to do that. I work alone. Besides, you should be here with your family, and to keep your eyes and ears open for any info that might help me."

"You already assigned me busy work to stay out of your way once today." He took a few steps toward her, and Alex angled her body to face him head-on. "We'll be stronger as a team." Her stance mirrored his. Feet firmly planted in the plush carpet, eyes leveled, and shoulders squared. They stood that way, in a silent debate, for one second, then five, then ten, until Alex threw her head back and laughed.

"Look at us, chests puffed out, feathers ruffled." Alex held her sides. Now he laughed too. It was a good feeling, a nice break from the heaviness. "Stronger as a team maybe, but there might not be enough room for our stubborn egos in one SUV."

"Don't forget Hank's," he said and gestured toward the bed, where the dog was desperately trying to reach his own tail. That started another fit of laughter. All the stress of the past few days had finally caught up, and he was slightly manic. Alex wiped away tears and threw the bag over her shoulder.

"What the hell? What's the worst thing that could happen?" Alex shot him a saucy smile and marched to the door.

As his eyes focused on her backside, showcased by skin-hugging jeans, he knew exactly the worst thing that could happen. He couldn't let the easy camaraderie weaken his defenses, just as he couldn't succumb to the unfairly seductive frame sauntering ahead of him.

Chapter Four

THROUGH THE GLASS door of Veterans' Services, Alex spotted the trademark swing of long blonde hair and smiled. She hadn't expected to run into her friend Lindsey, but she certainly wasn't disappointed by it. Hank saw her too and wiggled around in anticipation. When he was excited he was liable to knock something over with his slapping tail. Lindsey broke the conversation she was having with her husband Damien when Jay opened the door. He stepped back so Alex could walk in first.

Lindsey wrapped her in a sugar-scented hug the moment her feet touched the blue carpeted floor that nearly matched the chairs that lined the wall. Over her friend's shoulder she saw Lindsey's daughter Maris coloring at a pint-sized table with another toddler. Their sunny little heads and grinning faces were bent together as they wielded Crayolas like mad scientists. Her chest tightened, like a spider spinning wire webs around her sternum. In a different time, a different place either one of them could've been her sister Stephanie.

Suddenly, they were rocketing out of the tiny white chairs and stampeding toward Jay. She ordered Hank to sit when he started to go toward them, ready for an epic lick fest of two petite faces.

"Mister Jason! Do you have your balloons today?" the little girl shouted, her dimpled cheeks about to burst. Maris stood next to her, bouncing up on her tippy toes. Alex glanced at Jay and watched his hard face transform in front of her eyes. His expression softened and a genuine grin split over his lips. Oh yes, the scars on the right side of his face were still menacing, but for the kids he was instantly approachable and radiating warmth. He rubbed his hands together, reached in his pocket, and crouched down so he was eye level.

"Okay, go easy on me, Sadie. I'm going to try the elusive monkey." Jay shot a wink to Maris, while Sadie shrieked with delight and put both hands over her mouth.

If Alex tried to speak, she was sure no sound would pass through her lips. Speechless, she watched Jay twist and tangle the thin balloon until it was a hot-pink primate. The dog tilted its head from side to side with each move Jay made, as fascinated as Alex was by the process.

"Alex, your jaw is hanging open." Lindsey had moved closer and gave her a friendly hip bump.

"Who is this guy?" she whispered back with a chuckle, but it was strained. Seriously, was this the same deliciously dangerous man who was in her hotel room fifteen minutes ago?

"Ah. I see you haven't been introduced to the many sides

of Jay." Lindsey rested her elbow on Alex's shoulder. The weight of her arm gently pressing against her thin hoodie filled her head with college memories. Lindsey was bubbly and preppy while Alex was sullen and serious. At some point, Lindsey's constant cheer stopped annoying her and she got under her skin. They'd been friends ever since.

"What's it gonna be today, Maris? Giraffe? Frog? Another monkey?" His voice was playful, teasing. Sadie was making Hank's day by covering his slobbery face in tiny kid kisses.

Maris rolled her eyes and giggled. "A puppy!" The grin on Jay's face widened.

"We have a collection of about twenty," Damien said, letting her in on the joke.

"But some are wilted down to tiny, colorful nubs. Maris won't let us throw them away." Lindsey grinned.

Jay blew into a long purple balloon and began to transform the latex into a dog. When it was complete, he handed it over to Maris who kissed it on the nose.

"Sorry I can't stay and play longer, ladies," Jay said straightening from his crouch. "Alex, give me a second to grab a few things, run over some upcoming appointments with Damien."

"No problem. I'll hang here." She chose a chair that was far more comfortable than it appeared. Damien kissed Lindsey lightly on the mouth and he and Jay disappeared around a corner.

"How's he holding up?" Lindsey sank into the chair next to her. "He loves his family. It must be killing him."

"Like any survivor does. One foot in front of the other, always looking ahead." The fish tank bubbled in the background, and the little girls had gone silent as they resumed their coloring. "We'll find Luke." It was never possible to fully predict the outcome of a case, but Jay wouldn't stop until he found him. And just like with every missing person case that passed her desk, she wouldn't either.

Lindsey looped her arm through Alex's, gave it a squeeze. "You're awesome for helping him. Oh, Alex, look." Hank was slowly army crawling across the floor to the coloring table. For the next twenty minutes, they were entertained by the kids making paper crowns for her dog.

When the two men came back to the waiting room, Alex and Jay said their goodbyes. She patted her hip, and Hank reluctantly followed. They stepped outside and it was like walking into an industrial freezer. The cold seeped through the thin material of her shirt, chilling the bare skin underneath.

"So, balloon animals, huh? Would've pegged you for more of a shooting range, pool and beer kind of guy." She teased as they got back on the road bound for the Bourne Bridge. His laugh reverberated through the vehicle and a warmth spread through her stomach.

"Years ago, when I first started at Veterans' Services, my scars were still fresh. I don't care how most people perceive them, but I needed something to put the kids at ease. Balloons and stickers go a long way."

She eased on the brakes when the yellow light ahead changed to red. "You're a pretty decent human being." She dared to glance into his eyes, which were the same color as her favorite beverage, a double shot mocha latte. He was already staring at her and for a moment, she forgot to breathe. Silent acknowledgment filtered between them. The air grew heavy. How long had it been since she'd had a *moment* with someone? Her hands jolted against the wheel as the car behind them beeped. She swallowed and hit the gas as heat crept up her cheeks.

"Yeah, you don't suck either," Jay said, breaking the tension that had built up around them.

She had to rein in the smile that sought to bloom over her face. She'd always been different, maybe due to her childhood trauma, but did it make her a complete freak that his words gratified her more than any endearment or carefully crafted pickup line ever had? Completely annoyed with herself for letting her emotions get the better of her, Alex chose her favorite radio station. Jay's eyes twinkled in approval as Def Leppard cranked through the speakers.

They arrived in Foxboro at five o'clock and pulled up to the worn-out condo building ten minutes later. The lot was crowded, so she found a spot away from the building, put the car in park, and jumped out of the driver's side. Hank sat patiently as she secured his service vest that read *In Training*.

He was going to be a fantastic therapy dog.

"What unit are we headed to?" Jay asked as they met at the hood of the car, took in their surroundings, and walked hip to hip toward the entrance.

"Twelve." Gabe's research skills were impeccable, so she trusted they'd find Mr. Fletcher—if he was home.

"Good security." Jay gestured to the main door propped open with an overfilled trash can.

"They might be on to something. Who would want to come in with the smell of last week's rotting dinner?" Alex held her breath as Hank's tail slapped against the barrel. Even though it wasn't exactly clean, she didn't want to leave the building filthier than it already seemed.

"This is us," Jay said as he approached the door.

Alex tapped her knuckles against the frame in what she termed the "friendly neighbor knock."

They waited a moment, then the dull sound of footsteps was audible, and metal against metal as a sliding lock was released.

"Smart," Jay whispered under his breath. Again, the pleasure at his words rose up in her chest, and she shoved it back down. She didn't need anyone's approval.

The door opened, and Mr. Fletcher's eyes widened and darted between Alex, Jay, and the dog.

"Mr. Fletcher, we're sorry to hear you experienced some trouble with your 1970 Camaro. Could we come in and ask a few questions?" She studied him as he shifted about and dug his hands deep into the pockets of his baggy jeans. The hoodie he wore was a magnet for holes and stains.

"Already told the cops everything. Besides, the car was found." He started to shut the door, and she put the tip of her steel-toed boot on the threshold, just enough to stop it.

"Mr. Fletcher, I'd like to have a chat. Unless you'd rather discuss the ATM and gas station skimmers you placed last month. The state is cracking down. Stiffer penalties, more jail time. Let us in and I won't call the cops right here, right now." She stepped closer and watched Mr. Fletcher's face pale a few shades. They went through the kitchen to the living room, where the makings for a sandwich were loosely splayed out on the coffee table. The small space stank: stale cigarettes, unwashed dishes, and spilled mayonnaise.

She barely rested on the edge of the couch, afraid of what might be lurking beneath the cushions. Jay followed her lead, resting his elbows on his knees. He didn't say a word, but each time Mr. Fletcher's eyes passed over Jay's face, the career criminal shuddered. "Thank you for cooperating. It seems strange that someone you went to grade school with would steal your car." She waited patiently and watched.

Mr. Fletcher vigorously rubbed the tip of his nose. "What are you, dense? He had it out for me. The second he got booked and started serving time in Foxboro, I knew there would be trouble."

"Of course you did. Because you and Shane arranged it. He'd take the car, you'd report it stolen, and you'd get it back in a few weeks without the hassle of making arrangements to pick it up, because Shane's trip was a one-way deal. What did you get out of it? Wait." She held up a hand. "Let me guess, a little crack?" She could feel Jay's eyes on her for a moment, and then the sensation disappeared.

"You're crazy. I'm clean. You're fishing for info because you have none. Shane's no good, always out to get me into trouble," Mr. Fletcher said, and looked at both exit doors.

"I think you find that well enough on your own," Alex said. "You posted to Facebook on February sixth: *My boy Shane D. gets released from prison tomorrow*. Now tell us where he headed," she demanded.

His shoulders slumped, and he paced around the small, filthy living room. "He said something about the south. Some kind of mountain trail, and a cabin where he could stay with his son. That's all I know, I swear it."

Alex watched him for a moment and stood up, and Jay and Hank followed her lead. "My assistant's debit card got skimmed the week before Christmas. Couldn't afford to buy her kids gifts. It was a tough time for her, as she was newly divorced. Think of that next time you steal someone's hard-earned money, Mr. Fletcher."

Alex took care of her own. She'd actually had fun browsing the toy store as she filled up the cart for Nancy's twin boys, had them gift wrapped because it just wasn't her thing, and anonymously delivered by courier same-day.

Jay walked in front of her and was about to open the

front door when a fist banged on the other side.

"Police. Open up." There was another rap on the door.

Jay turned the knob. Two police officers were waiting on the other side.

"Officers, the floor is yours." Alex whipped around at the feral scream behind her.

"You bitch!" Mr. Fletcher screamed. "You said you wouldn't call the cops. I'll sue you. I'll bring you down!"

"No," she said shooting him a hard look. "I said I wouldn't call right here, right now. And I didn't. I called at a rest stop twenty minutes ago."

"Thanks, Alexandra." Cliff Martin, who she'd known for a while, stepped in and took stock of the condo.

"How did you know?" Jay asked once they were back in the SUV with Hank looking out the window in the back seat.

"I didn't. Gabe checked out his Facebook page. People post the darndest things. Sometimes, people can't help but brag about their bad behavior. I just took a chance that he really did what he said in the post." They were silent for a few miles, letting Iron Maiden and AC/DC make all the noise.

"So, this Gabe." Jay looked over, and her stomach did the obnoxious summersault thing again. "You guys a thing?"

"Gabe's a great guy, but no. I don't do relationships. Easy, no strings—that's more my pace. And he might be just a bit pretty for my personal taste, but a hell of a computer whiz." She dared to take another look at him, and the sly smirk gave her a jolt.

"What are you saying, Red?" He tilted his head, eyes mischievous. He was all male. Rough and scarred. She'd seen the bold tattoos that illustrated his corded muscles. The thought of them made her throat dry. He was built like a giant oak: tall, strong, sturdy. Yet, he crouched on the ground and made balloon animals with gentle hands.

She was playing a dangerous game. Alex knew it, but she shot him a sideways glance, felt her lips curve. "I go for someone a little more…rugged." She let the words hang, and saw the double-dare-you look in his eyes.

She wouldn't, or at least she shouldn't give in to those challenging eyes. Jay would be like chicken pox—once you scratched the itch, you wouldn't be able to stop yourself from doing it again.

Chapter Five

AFTER THEY WERE done ruining Fletcher's day, they backtracked to the Cape armed with the information they needed to confidently start the drive south. Alex dropped Jay off at the beach parking lot, where he'd left his truck parked. Even though it would be the dead of night when they left, they decided two hours was enough time to pack their things, make a few arrangements, and begin the search. He'd run home and pack a few essentials while Alex phoned her office, gathered her things from the hotel room, and got the dog's food and supplies.

He put the truck in drive and tapped his fingers impatiently against the wheel as he waited for a string of cars to pass. Jay pulled out onto the main road and cranked the heat. It did little to chase away the cold hatred in his heart for Shane and what he had put his sister through. His jaw tightened. If only he had known Shane forced himself on Amy, he wouldn't be alive to have kidnapped Luke. How Alex had uncovered what happened after fifteen minutes with his sister, after he'd lived under the same roof with her half his life, made his stomach turn. How had he missed the signs?

The glow of streetlamps illuminated the shops and businesses that lined downtown Chatham. Some were boarded up for the season, like the penny candy shop and Sal's Seafood Shack, which churned out some of the best lobster rolls and clam strips on the Cape. As soon as the weather warmed up, their sleepy town would be brimming with tourists eager to buy sea-themed knickknacks, stretch out on the sandy beaches, and tour historic lighthouses. He loved all those things, too but it was walking along the boardwalk over miles of marshland, through tall, golden rods of sea grass and out to the ocean that always called to him.

His other sister's house wasn't far from his, and if the lights were on, he'd swing by to ask how Amy was doing. Sure enough, the windows were washed in a soft glow, so he slowed the truck and took a left into the driveway. Outside the truck, the gentle scent of pine and sea salt hung in the air. Before he made it to the door, it swung open and his other sister Courtney stood in the frame. She pulled him into a hard hug at the threshold.

"Don't you dare blame yourself. I know you are because that's what I've been doing ever since Amy told me what happened." She shook her head and raked her fingers through her long blonde hair. At five foot eight, Courtney was far taller than his mother or Amy. She'd gone to college on a basketball scholarship and had a killer slam dunk.

"Don't know how we missed it, but once I get my hands

on—"

"Shut up." Courtney cut him off and spun around in the hallway. "None of that macho Marine crap. As much as I'd love to see Shane writhe, I'm not going to let my only brother wind up in jail—so just don't."

Jay rolled his eyes to the ceiling and followed her into the kitchen. When Courtney was in a mood, it was best to let things ride, and right now he couldn't blame her. She yanked open the refrigerator, and the condiments lining the door rattled.

"I need a beer." She pulled a bottle of winter ale from a six-pack and popped the top off with a mermaid-shaped opener on the kitchen counter.

He raised an eyebrow "Huh." Courtney didn't go for whimsical details. Jay glanced around the room. There was a glittery vase filled with sand and shells on the dining room table, and he shot a smirk at Courtney who blew out a breath, sending a few strands of her hair up and out. Jay poked his head into the living room, and his smile widened.

"There's decorative pillows on your couch," he teased.

"I'm aware, as it's my couch. Beer?" Courtney reached back into the fridge.

"Throw me a soda." She tossed up a can, and he caught it with his left hand. "So, when did Ashley move in?"

Courtney sighed. "Don't tell Mom yet. I know she wouldn't care—I'm thirty-three. It's the onslaught of questions. When are you going to buy a ring? When can we shop for wedding dresses? We're just trying to move slow."

A laugh roared out of him. "Slow? You've been with Ashley so long she's practically another sister. Just buy the damn ring."

Courtney turned, but Jay still caught the suppressed smile on her face. "Maybe I will." She sat at the table, stretched out her legs, and slugged back the beer. He hadn't realized how bad he wanted one, but Alex might need him to drive so sugary-sweet soda was the only thing on the menu.

"Any new updates?" Courtney asked.

"Shane might be headed south. We're leaving tonight. How was Amy holding up?" Jay took a sip of his drink and bubbles burst over his tongue.

"As expected. Mom came over around three so I could come home and get some work done, but I'm going to pack a bag and sleep over. She shouldn't be alone and Ashley doesn't get back from her business trip until tomorrow, so it's okay. Wait—did you say we?"

"I'm tagging along with the investigator. Two brains will be better than one, even though she's razor sharp." Jay glanced at the clock. It was almost time to get going.

Courtney smirked. "How well do you know her? Amy said you were friends, but you've never mentioned her." She tilted her head with raised brows. *Damn.* His sisters meant well, but they had a tendency to meddle.

Jay shrugged. He knew Alex had the softest lips that he'd ever kissed and that there was a small scar on her left hip, but he didn't really know anything about her at all. Maybe the ride south would change that.

"Alex is more of a friend of a friend, but she's trustworthy. You don't have to worry." Jay lifted the can to his lips and took a sip.

"I wasn't worried about her work. I was thinking of my big brother." Courtney's lips curved into a tired smirk and Jay froze with the can in his left hand midway to his lips.

"Come on. What's there to worry about?" Jay scoffed. He leaned back and rested his outer ankle on his knee.

"Just the way Amy told me about your visit this morning…seemed like there might be something between you two," she said. The motion censored hall light switched off, darkening the room. "Hey, Google. Turn on the living room lights." Two corner lamps illuminated the space. "Now, that's one thing Ashley convinced me to buy that I don't want to return. Sorry, back to Amy."

Jay cleared his throat and adjusted the collar of his shirt. "You must have misread her," he mumbled.

"Maybe. But I'm not misreading you. Talking about her makes you uncomfortable. What happened?" Courtney leaned forward, and a glint shone in her eyes.

"Nothing I'm discussing with one of my sisters." Jay put both feet on the floor, ready to stand up. It was time to go throw some things in his duffel bag and wait for Alex.

"Jay!" Courtney slapped her hands against her knees. "You hooked up with her. When?" She stood up and took the empty can from his hand and tossed it in the recycling bin with her bottle.

"Come on, don't make this weird." He didn't even know if hooked up was the appropriate word. They'd locked lips for a few minutes after she offered to drive him home from Lindsey and Damien's cottage one night. He sensed it would've gone further, but the kiss rocked him just enough that he eased back.

"It's kind of a big deal. It's been a long time since you broke it off with Becky." Courtney's voice dropped. It had been a tough time for all of them, and his family never understood why he'd ended the relationship with his long-time girlfriend. It wasn't something he cared to talk about. The air in the room stilled and Jay rocked on the balls of his feet.

"I don't want you to get hurt," Courtney continued. "Amy mentioned Alex just seems really tough, independent. I always pictured you with someone more girl-next-doorsy…someone—"

"Someone like Becky," Jay finished for her. It irked him that after four years his family still made subtle comments about her.

"Well, yes. I guess I'll never understand. You'd planned to come home and propose. She really cared for you." Courtney shook her head slightly, and Jay's throat tightened up. In his family's eyes, he'd forever be the callous one who had left poor, sweet Becky, but it was better than explaining how it felt when he went to his best friend's house that day and found them together.

"I'll let you know as soon as there's an update on Luke." Jay kissed Courtney on the top of the head.

"When you get back, you're coming with me to the jeweler's." Courtney cocked one hip against the counter and smiled.

"Damn straight," he said and walked out of the kitchen and through the front door.

Chapter Six

Alex put her car in park outside of Jay's cottage and took a giant gulp of her extra-large coffee. Ordering it at the drive-through window had been an embarrassment. By the time Alex rattled off what she wanted, they might've handed a hot fudge sundae covered in candy out the window, but the triple mocha swirl did wonders for her mood and would keep her awake on the road. She'd added a plain donut to her order to share with Hank, who'd left a layer of drool over her back seat at the mere sight of it. He was sleeping soundly, and every so often his paws would kick against the seat as he dreamed of chasing his Frisbee.

Maybe if she traveled with someone more often, she would've thought to pick him up something, too. The logistics of the trip were nagging at her. Alex was giving it too much thought. Did she need to make small talk for the nine-hundred-mile drive? Entertain him? It would be so much easier to go on her own. To stop, eat, and sleep when she needed to. Alex took another sip from the paper cup and nearly sighed as the hot, sweet coffee trailed down her throat.

Then the front door slammed, and the porch light

flashed on. She looked toward the house, and Jay waved to her as he came down the steps. He'd changed into different jeans and a sweatshirt. He carried a black duffel in his hand. Her eyes clung to his hulking shadow for more than a few seconds under the guise of her tinted windows and the night's sky.

"Hey, stranger." Jay opened the passenger side door, slid in, and tossed his bag over the seat. The fresh, invigorating scent of his soap, mixed with the smell of mocha coffee, reminded her of mint chocolate chip ice cream.

"Let's hit the road," Alex said and pulled out onto the street. "Your work must be flexible to be able to take off like this." She glanced over her left shoulder before easing out onto the main road.

"They're understanding, and I've been with the organization for a few years now. But it's really Damien who makes the difference. Our families are really comfortable with him, so he can easily fill the gaps," Jay said, chin held high and shoulders thrust back against the seat. Lindsey mentioned Jay had been the one to recruit Damien when the two men became friends. Clearly it was working out well. Alex drove toward the Bourne Bridge. It paid to leave at night when the traffic was less heavy.

"Damien seems like a good guy. And he treats Lindsey like a queen." Alex was starting to relax a bit. It wouldn't be the end of the world if they drove in silence for a few miles or talked the whole way.

"Yeah, and he got pretty lucky with Lindsey and Maris. She's a cute kid." Jay smiled, and it was genuine.

"I didn't peg you as someone who would have a soft spot for kids until I saw you twisting up balloon animals. You're good with her." Kids wouldn't fit into Alex's lifestyle, and after the pain of losing her sister, she'd be a nervous wreck to have that kind of responsibility, but it didn't mean she couldn't appreciate a strong man with a compassionate nature.

"They're funny. Unfiltered. Completely honest. I appreciate that. You would think it's mostly men who go to Veterans' Services but I get to work with a lot of kids, wives, grandparents. The kids ask questions most adults would shy away from." Jay was looking out the window, and Alex stole a glance at his face. Sitting this way, all she could see was smooth skin and a firm jaw.

"Like your scars, you mean?" Alex eased her foot on the brake and slowed down behind a few cars coming to a stop.

"Yeah. There are times a kid will come in with a parent who's struggling, one with far graver injuries than I have, but it seems to put them at ease, to see my face, to see I'm on my feet, that I'm working, that life goes on." Jay tapped his fingers on the window ridge. Maybe he didn't like talking about it, and maybe she'd brought it up because she wanted him to know it didn't bother her, but his scars didn't seem to faze him either way. He carried himself like a Marine, with straight shoulders and an assertive gait.

Traffic started moving again, as she struggled to find the right thing to say. "A stamp of courage." Alex bit the corner of her lip, and Jay chuckled.

"Something like that." He grinned at her, and Alex's heart forgot to beat for a second. It was a feeling she didn't appreciate. Alex was a lone wolf. She didn't need anyone, and she didn't want anyone to complicate her life. "Anyway, I'm not here to invade your space, but if you want to swap, I can drive if you get tired or whatever. Just say the word." Jay leaned back a bit in the seat as Alex took the exit to the highway, merged into the left lane, and hit the gas.

"Thanks." She wouldn't take him up on the offer, but it was a nice gesture. They drove for a couple of hours before making a pit stop, getting a coffee refill, and getting back on the road. Around Connecticut icy rain began to spit down from the clouds and by the time they hit New York, it was coming down in a steady drizzle. Jay's head was bent down, scrolling through his phone.

"Severe storm warning for all of New York State," Jay said. Alex felt his eyes on her. If she were alone, Alex would just press on.

"What's it calling for?" She briefly took her eyes off the nearly deserted road. Most people were resting their heads on pillows. She could make out the faint outline of ominous clouds in the night's sky.

"Destructive wind and torrential rain. Looks like the works." Jay rested his phone on his lap.

"Any objections to pushing forward?" It was important they make good time. The longer they delayed, the further Shane and Luke could be moving away.

"Not one." Jay's mouth curved into a grin and Alex shot him a smile. For a moment, the reasons why she was so apprehensive about company vanished from her mind. Instead of just doing her job, it was like she was part of something bigger.

"I was hoping you'd say that." As if to call them foolish, the sky opened up, and a blanket of rain beat down on the windows. A heavy coat of Rain-X and newly replaced windshield wipers took care of most of it, so visibility wasn't awful.

"Talk about timing." Jay chuckled. He was so affable. It was one of the reasons Alex was drawn to him when they met. Clearly, he'd had troubles, but it didn't stop him from smiling or cracking a joke. He hadn't let life knock him down when he came home from war injured. A couple of cars had moved into the breakdown lane of the highway to wait out the worst of the rain, but they kept moving. Then the car ahead of them skidded, and she jerked the wheel to the left to move into another lane.

"Shit," Alex said.

"There's an underpass up ahead if you want to pull over. Get the car out of it." Jay's voice was calm, completely unfazed by the stormy surroundings.

"I don't mind a little rain. It's my engine light." Alex

swore again when the dashboard lights dimmed. The steering wheel jerked once in her hands, and the car dropped to a crawl, even though her foot was firmly planted on the gas pedal. They made it a few feet from the cover of the underpass before the car stopped. Hank stirred from his deep slumber and poked his head in between the front seats.

"Want to pop the hood? I'll take a look," Jay said, opened his door, and slipped out into the dark before she could say a word. Alex told the dog to stay and jumped out of the SUV. Her feet hit the pavement with a splash, and cold rain slicked over her arms, face, and neck. Alex joined Jay at the front of the car and leaned over to get a closer look through the stream of light coming from Jay's cell phone. The battery cables were both connected as they should be.

"This car is no more than six months old, so it can't be the battery," she mumbled and pinched the bridge of her nose.

"It could be a lot of things, but nothing seems to jump out." White puffs of air came out of Jay's mouth as he spoke. The cold, bitter wind whipped around them and she jammed her hands deeper into her sweatshirt pocket.

Alex sighed. "Oh, well. Let's get back in and call triple A." The rain picked up, flogging them with heavy gusts. Jay slammed down the hood, and they both jumped back in the SUV. Alex made the call, was given a wait time that seemed reasonable given the weather and the time of morning. Jay had reached over the back seat while she was on the phone and rummaged through his bag. Now, his hand was outstretched toward her, offering up a blue wicking towel.

Alex took it and ran it over her skin. "You're better prepared than I am."

"Usually they're only useful for runs. Not sure when I thought I'd have the chance to do that, but I packed them anyway." Jay wiped his brow with another towel he'd pulled from the bag. Great. So, they shared a favorite pastime too, or at least powered through the same activity.

"I always run in the morning to wake up. That and drink an enormous amount of coffee." Alex squeezed pieces of her sopping hair with the towel until it wasn't dripping on her shoulders. In high school, the pot and pills and alcohol only dragged her down deeper, but she'd used them as a way to cope with the loss and guilt she faced. Until her gym teacher busted her with a dime bag, and in lieu of ratting her out made her run laps after school for a week. Running had become a sort of therapy to her. When her shoes were slapping the pavement, Alex could focus on her breath, the road in front of her, and leave her thoughts behind.

"That I can see." Jay's voice was playful and his eyes locked on the second giant cup of the day.

"Everyone has a vice." Alex picked up the cup. The coffee had gone cold long ago, but she drank it anyway. Her vices would've been far more detrimental if it weren't for that gym teacher. Had he known what he was doing, or was it sheer luck that had saved her from herself?

As if reading her mind, Jay said, "It could be worse." And he grinned again. Jeez, she liked his grin.

"What's yours? Running, eating an apple a day, three square meals?" Alex was starting to enjoy his company, and the torrents of rain beating down eliminated all visibility from within the car leaving them closed off to the outside.

"Sitting on the beach with no one around for miles, summer ale, redheads." He said the last word slowly, let it hang. The air in the car changed. It was the first time he'd flirted with her since the brief hookup.

"That would make for a good singles column in the newspaper," Alex said dryly but sent him a smile all the same.

Jay laughed. There it was again—that tough resolve despite what he'd been through. "Has anyone used those since the seventies? Might make a good About Me section on Tinder."

Alex grimaced. Thousands of people met their significant others on those sites, but in a world where a child could get snatched from their front yard, it didn't seem exactly safe to her. "If you're looking for someone, you'd do better hanging around at a bar or beachside."

"I don't know, the last woman I kissed scurried off without leaving her number. Left me kind of jaded." A smirk played around the corners of his lips and there was a gleam in his eyes.

Alex's throat was suddenly dry, and electricity snapped in

the car like the lightning outside. He was staring at her, waiting for a response. The smile was gone now. It would be easy to inch over and kiss him to replace the suddenly uncomfortable situation with something physical.

"It wasn't personal. I don't date as a rule. There's too much going on at the firm. Besides, with you, things were…different, and I—" The knock on the window startled them both. Alex rolled it down and was face-to-face with a tow truck driver.

"Bad deal to break down in this." The flashlight in his hands illuminated the middle-aged man with wisps of gray hair over his forehead and round, red cheeks. He laughed into the storm.

"Bad deal to have to pull our sorry asses to safety," Alex said, and this time, the man clutched his hands to his stomach when he laughed, making the stream of light bounce up and down.

"Go ahead and wait in the tow truck. The shop is right next to a Hertz but it won't open until seven. There's a motel across the street. Nothing fancy but it's not a dive." He pulled the zipper of his yellow jacket higher over his chin.

"We'll probably need to take a rental in the morning and come back for this one on the return trip." Alex took her purse, her own duffel bag, the hard, black case that secured her Glock .40, and pushed against the wind to open the driver's side door. When she did, she was assaulted by rain. She leashed Hank, who lumbered out of the back seat, unphased by the storm. The tow truck driver glanced at the dog with wide eyes and muttered something under his breath.

It was a thirty-minute ride to the motel across from the auto shop, with Hank tightly packaged between them like a pressed panini. By the time they got there, Alex was stir-crazy thinking of how much ground Shane and Luke could've covered during this period. Jay must have felt it too because he was quieter than he had been the whole trip.

At least there was a car rental right next to the shop, but their hands were tied until daybreak. The driver rounded the corner and pointed across the street to where the SUV would be serviced. It was an easy walk across the road. Alex was used to driving long distances, sometimes at odd hours, but when she slid out of the tow truck she had to stifle a yawn. Quietly, they unloaded the car, went to the front desk and made two separate transactions for their rooms at an hourly rate. Just enough for a few hours' sleep, then they'd be back on the trail.

"What room are you?" Jay asked as they walked away from the desk and back outside. The overhang protected them from the heaviest rain as they circled the building, but sprays carried by the wind still snuck over them.

"Fifteen. You?" Alex skirted around a puddle that had risen up in a dip in the concrete and bumped Jay's shoulder.

"Sixteen," Jay answered as he put his palm on the middle of her back so she wouldn't trip.

"Looks like we're neighbors then," Alex said as they came to the two whitewashed doors. "Let's set our alarms for six thirty. I can settle up at the tow place and we can grab the first rental available. We don't want to lose any more time." Alex looked over at Jay who nodded in response, eyes clouded. Of course, Jay knew that—it was his nephew after all, and his sister who was counting on them.

Alex pulled out her plastic key card. As she was about to insert it into the lock, Jay turned toward her.

"Alex, about what you said in the car before the tow company showed. What was different?" Jay's voice was so rugged, and it sent a shiver up her spine.

She didn't need to give him any reason to pursue her, but she wasn't a liar either, and he'd asked. "I might've enjoyed myself…too much."

A boyish smile bloomed on his face, and he glanced at the floor, then up at her again.

"Night, then," he said, put the key card in the door, and disappeared inside looking like he'd won the lottery. Alex stood for a moment under the motel's overhang. She wasn't sure what she'd expected, but it wasn't for him to go into his room. Alex certainly shouldn't be disappointed—these were her rules she was playing by after all—but she was.

Chapter Seven

At six thirty, the alarm on Jay's cell phone went off. He slid his legs over the side of the bed, and his feet touched the inn's worn green carpet. The few hours of rest had refreshed him, and he was eager to get back on the road. Had Shane found Luke shelter last night, or had he forced him to sleep in the car as they got further and further away? A million things could go wrong with an impulsive man at the wheel, who was probably very paranoid about abducting his estranged son. Jay pushed it out of his head and moved across the dimly lit room.

He had to duck his head when he walked through the bathroom doorway. Jay clasped the shower knob, cranked it on hot, and sighed as a weak spray of water came out of the faucet. It heated to lukewarm at best, and he had to crouch down to avoid hitting the showerhead. Jay's mind wandered to what Alex had said a few hours before: *I might've enjoyed myself…too much.*

Maybe his sisters were right; maybe there was a little spark between him and Alex. Who was he kidding? Ever since they'd sat across from each other during dinner at

Damien and Lindsey's house, the chemistry between them had sizzled. Still, he wasn't looking for commitments or promises he wasn't emotionally ready to make.

Jay slipped out of the shower and wrapped one of the small white towels around his waist. A knock echoed dully through the room, and he yanked on a pair of jeans over his damp legs and went to answer the door. Alex stood outside, wearing a hoodie and sweatpants, her hair tousled around her face. God, she was adorable like this—more relaxed, more vulnerable. Hank barreled forward and placed two heavy front paws on his shoulders. He laughed when the dog tried to lap its tongue over his entire face and he cringed as the dog's breath assaulted his nose.

"We're working on that." Alex stepped inside and closed the door.

"Might I recommend a toothbrush?" he said as the dog panted inches from his face.

"Hey, everyone gets morning breath—even handsome Hank. I meant jumping up on people. Anyway, my shower's broken. Mind if I use yours? I won't take long." Alex took a step closer.

"Have at it, but fair warning—it's like standing under a semi-cool watering can." Jay stepped back and the dog's front paws returned to the worn carpet. Alex went straight to the bathroom, and within a few moments, the hum of the shower sounded faintly through the closed door. Jay tossed his things into his duffel bag and tried not to think of water dripping over a naked Alex. The subtle curves and hard lines of her body were still etched in his mind. It had been one hell of a night and they hadn't even slept together.

True to her word, Alex reappeared a few minutes later, dressed and ready to go, with her damp hair brushed back away from her face. Water had tempered the vibrant, fiery red and darkened her strands to auburn, illuminating her creamy skin.

"You weren't kidding about that shower." She walked across the room wearing jeans and a T-shirt, holding her other clothes in her left hand. When she got near, he caught the burst of lime, and the scent of something sugary and fresh. "Did you get some rest?" Alex asked as she slowed a few steps away from him.

"I can sleep just about anywhere, at any time." Jay had put on a T-shirt while Alex was in the shower and finished gathering his things.

"I guess you learned to sleep when and where you could, huh?"

"In boot camp, we got eight hours, but after deployment, it was another beast entirely. Sometimes we'd get our sleep in fifteen-minute increments. It's one of those basic things you take for granted until it's a luxury. But you're the one who's been driving—what about you?" Jay glanced at her lips. They were just full enough, and unpainted they were the color of raspberries.

"Enough to safely operate a vehicle," she assured him.

Alex seemed to be standing closer, and her bottom lip opened ever so slightly. The only sound in the room was the vibration of the ancient heater. Jay's nerve endings tingled as he looked into her wide eyes. The tips of his fingers tingled, and he could barely constrain his desire to touch her. What kind of uncle was he to think that when Luke was still missing?

Alex cleared her throat and the moment was lost. "I'll get my stuff and we can go get a rental," she croaked out in a hoarse voice. He could tell she wanted him too.

When he stepped out of the room, she was already waiting. They crossed the busy road that separated the hotel from the car rental company. A gentleman who wore a neatly ironed shirt and tan slacks was just sliding his key into the lock. He looked over his shoulder at them and his lips flattened into a hard line, clearly miffed at having such early customers. They stood in the waiting area as the man booted up his desktop computer. After a few moments, Alex walked up to the front desk and began completing the paperwork for the car. When it came time to put a credit card on file, Jay stepped forward and slid his across the desk before Alex could say a word. He wasn't about to let her foot the bill for this entire expedition.

"You didn't have to do that, Jay," she said as they exited the building with keys to a four-door sedan.

"I didn't have to—I needed to. You're jumping through hoops to help me out. To help my family and nephew. It's appreciated more than you can imagine." Jay lowered his chin to look at her as they crossed the parking lot to the car.

"It's my job." Alex popped the trunk of a silver vehicle and dropped her bags inside.

"A job is something you get compensated for." Jay swung the duffel in the trunk and closed it shut.

"I do in other ways." Alex's voice was solemn and her face unreadable. Jay got a sick stir in his gut. When Amy told him Alex worked on all missing children cases pro bono, he was a little baffled. What was her reason to help families find their loved ones without charging a dime? He fought between curiosity and caution. Alex had put up walls and he had an unrelenting urge to break them down.

He let it go until they got in the car and onto the open road. Traffic was heavy with morning commuters, and Alex tapped her thumb on the steering wheel as they crawled down the highway.

"Is it okay if I get personal for a second?" Jay's eyes flickered over to her. She did that tensing up thing again.

"If it's not, I'll let you know." The rigid line of her mouth said it all, but he decided to ask regardless.

"Why do you do what you do? Help families. It seems you could be making a big profit off missing persons—and it wouldn't be unethical or wrong. It's a job, and from where I'm sitting a hell of a lot of work. Why free?"

Alex looked away from the road briefly to cast her vivid eyes on him. Their gilded depths spoke of loss and pain. She didn't answer right away and for a moment, it seemed she wasn't going to respond at all.

"Some PIs charge hand over fist to locate a missing person. They know families are desperate, vulnerable and will open their wallets, but some can't afford to pay. That's where I come in. No one should have to make that kind of financial decision. Help should be available to those who need it most." Alex's voice was edged with anger and an abrupt finality that told him she wasn't ready to open up. He was used to waiting, drawing out information slowly as trust was built—and Alex wasn't quite there yet.

She seemed to hide behind a brisk, no-nonsense exterior, but she was so much more. It was in the way she doted on her giant dog, babying him like a child. Or the way she'd looked at Maris with such affection. It was in the way she'd kissed him so fiercely, giving every bit of herself to the moment. Something painful had happened to her and all he wanted to do was soothe the ache.

They drove quietly for the next couple hours. Jay sensed Alex needed the silence. That telling him even a little bit about her drive to find missing kids left her drained. If only they were stopped, he'd reach over and gather her up in his arms. Would she let him hold her close for just a moment? Perhaps that was part of the problem. When you refused to lean on anyone, it was easy to forget how. Jay had been fantasizing about sleeping with her, but now the situation was quite clear. Alex didn't need a lover. She needed a friend.

BY THE TIME they made it across the Maryland line, Alex was dying to get out of the car. She'd spent too much time in her own head the past few hours after Jay had asked about her missing children cases—the most crucial component of her entire operation. It was the reason she'd hired Gabe to focus on cheating spouses, corrupt stakeholders, and employees who were trying to beat the system. She had never told anyone the whole truth. That her baby sister, who was all smiles and songs and light, was gone because of her. If only Alex could change that split-second decision to run inside the house, Stephanie wouldn't have been snatched from the yard. Even mentioning her work with families of missing children was more information than she usually volunteered. Jay's trustworthy and kind nature just made him easy to talk to.

The rest stop sign came up fast and Alex veered into the right lane to take the exit ramp. She pulled into the first gas station she saw, chose a vacant parking spot, and killed the engine.

"I'm dying for a coffee," Alex said and unbuckled. She should stick to water or a soft drink. Between mulling over the past and the gallons of coffee she'd consumed, her stomach was churning.

"Hey," Jay said softly and touched her arm. "You okay?" Alex didn't deserve the compassion in his voice. She deserved nothing after letting her sister get abducted. His tender tone made her eyes sting.

"I'm fine." She instantly regretted the snap in her tone but oh, how revisiting that horrific day still hurt. Sometimes it snuck out of nowhere and slammed her in the chest, making her heart pound and her stomach tangle into sickening knots. The remorse was so overwhelming at times that she had to sit on the floor and tuck her head between her knees until the feeling passed. Jay's hand slid down her arm as Alex slipped out of the car and got Hank out of the back seat. Alex fastened his service vest so he could follow them into the store. She stepped up onto the curb and swung open the glass door plastered with signs for ninety-nine cent hot dogs and cigarettes.

Hank instantly began sniffing the air, but Alex was pleased he didn't tug on his leash to get to the warmer of rotating franks. Alex used the restroom, which was not made for a person and a dog of Hank's size. After she'd splashed some water on her face, she and Hank circled the small store in search of coffee. Jay was filling a cup at the Slurpee machine, which made her feel slightly better about dumping sugar and cream into her drink. She tossed a few bottled waters into the crook of her arm from the refrigerator that lined the wall and strode up to the cash register. A cashier with an intense unibrow grunted out a hello and started ringing up her items. Alex nearly sighed in frustration when Jay plopped his frozen drink on the counter and slid over a twenty. The cashier looked up, locked his eyes on Jay's face, and took a step back.

She couldn't blame the man for being startled. Jay looked formidable at times given his size and build, not to mention the jagged scars over one side of his face. He wore them so well, it only added to his appeal. He was a man you wanted on your side when danger came, someone who would have your back.

She raised her brows to the ceiling and back down to Jay. "You seriously have to stop doing that. I can pay my own way." He just gave her a friendly shoulder bump, and Alex made a show of rolling her eyes. She reached into her back pocket and pulled out a photo of Luke and another one of Shane. She put it down in front of the cashier. "Seen these people?" she asked. His brow instantly bunched in the middle of his forehead and Alex knew she'd hit the mark. Everyone stopped at the first rest area after a long strip of highway.

The cashier jammed his finger against the picture so hard, the countertop display of mints and wildlife lighters jolted and spilled forward. Alex caught the Bics, ones with roaring grizzly bears painted on them, and placed them back on the table. "That's him." He yelled something into the back room using a different language that Alex couldn't quite place, but the tone said it all. Seriously pissed off. A younger man who was the spitting image of the cashier, complete with the brow, appeared from the back. The cashier slid the picture of Shane over, still tapping the image as he rattled off an incoherent string of words that Alex could only assume were obscenities.

"I take it you've seen them," Jay said with a grim voice. It was easy to see by the reaction that Shane had caused trouble at the store. Was Luke's father getting desperate? Had he cracked?

The younger man turned his dark eyes toward them. "He stole from my father's store. Food, drinks, lighters. This man pushed him down when he tried to stop that thief from leaving."

Alex stole a quick look at Jay. The muscles in his neck were corded and his jaw set. "He'll answer for it. In the meantime, I'll settle up with you; but first, did you see the boy?" The older cashier shook his head no and Jay's shoulders dipped. "That man is my nephew's biological father and a toxin to society. He abducted my nephew, and the information you just provided gives us an idea of their course." The cashier's face softened as Jay took out his wallet and Alex slipped the photo back into her pocket.

"When did this happen?" Alex asked, keeping her voice neutral.

"Wednesday. Around midnight." The cashier stepped back a little and crossed his arms over his chest.

"Thanks for your help." Now they had something more to go on as they continued the search. "Meet you outside," Alex said to Jay. The door chimed as she walked through, and she unlocked the rental and got inside the car. Alex scrolled through her email as she waited for Jay. After a few moments, she caught his form out of the corner of her eyes. When he sat down and settled in, Alex angled her body to face him. "If Shane ripped off one store and got away with it, chances are he'll do it again. You can't go paying for his indiscretions at every stop you make."

Jay shook his head and let out a long breath. "They didn't see Luke. What if Shane dumped him off somewhere or worse?"

"I know this isn't easy, but we have to remain focused on logic. If Shane's stealing food and supplies it supports Fletcher's statement that he might be bringing Luke to a cabin in the mountains. Now it's only a matter of time before we locate them or Shane is caught, by us or the cops. We're hot on their trail now—only two days behind."

"You're right. Thanks for talking me down." Jay ran his hand over the top of his head.

"Let's go find them." Alex looked over her shoulder, then reversed. Instead of getting on the highway, she drove to a few more points of interest Shane might have stopped at and struck out.

The last stop they made was a fast-food joint. No one recognized the pictures but they didn't leave empty-handed. Alex's stomach growled loudly as the smell of French fries and burgers rose up from the brown paper bags they carried. Outside, they sat at a wooden picnic table nestled in the shade of a white oak tree. It was still cool out, but much warmer than it had been in Massachusetts, and it was a great opportunity for Hank to roll around in the grass.

"I feel tenser about everything," Jay said as he opened the bag and peeled back the yellow wrapper on his sandwich.

Alex took a sip of her drink and the sweet lemon-lime bubbles slid down her throat. "Don't. Chances are they got back on I-95 and are heading further south. I think we should keep moving forward and hit up other gas stations and convenience stores right off the highway. If Shane's looking to knock off another store, he'll want easy on, easy off. Honestly, if he hurt or killed Luke I don't think he'd be buying supplies. He'd be doing his best to get out of the country."

Jay's hands paused as he lifted the cheeseburger to his mouth. His face looked pained. Dammit—she hadn't meant to be that blunt. "Sorry. This is rough on you and I'm not making it easier with my poor choice of words. My outlook tends to be a bit cynical, but I do feel good about the information we've found."

"I like to keep my glass half full, but unfortunately this situation is different." Jay lifted his soda and the sleeve of his shirt crept up revealing the bottom of his tattoo. She had to take a sip of her own drink when the fry inside her mouth turned to sawdust. She recalled he had some ink from their night together—one that almost ended with her sleeping with someone for the first time in years. It was an eagle rising over the world, and it only enhanced the masculinity of his body. Jay caught her staring, smiled.

She nodded toward his upper arm. "What does it say?" He lifted his shirtsleeve higher. "Death before dishonor," Alex read out loud. "There's not many honorable people left in this world." She dipped a fry in ketchup to tear her gaze away from the defined muscle of his bicep and the tattoo that made him look just a little wicked and dangerous.

"I don't think you're hanging around the right people, Alex." The way Jay said her name sent a delicious shiver down her spine. "There's still good in this world. You just have to open your eyes to it." Jay crumpled the empty wrapper in his hand and tossed it in the brown bag.

Of course, he would say that. His comment left her slightly miffed. Jay hadn't experienced how truly evil people could be. Except, she realized, he had. Alex studied his face and her defenses softened. "I don't hang out with many people at all," she muttered. Why had she said that? "I mean, I have Lindsey." Ugh. She sounded so lame, but honestly, she kind of was. Alex didn't date and her social calendar was typically that of a shut-in. She spent long hours at work, poring over cases, and making her business successful. It didn't matter that now the business was well established and had earned a stellar reputation. Alex still put in too many hours to fill up the void of loneliness.

"Aren't we friends?" Jay asked with a twinkle in his soft eyes.

She couldn't help but smile. "I don't make personal relationships with clients, but I think I could swing a friend." Alex popped another fry in her mouth and licked the salt off her finger. When she looked up, Jay was staring at her with a hungry expression.

"I think we're way past that point. If I remember correctly, we were very nearly as personal as it gets," Jay said with an irritating diplomacy in his voice.

The food Alex was chewing went down the wrong way, and she coughed a few times. Her cheeks heated. Since when had she become bashful? "Yes…well. I've got a lot of emotional baggage. I'm not exactly in a position for anything else."

"So, you've got the emotional baggage and I have the physical." Jay gestured toward his face. "Together we're like a whole person." His voice was teasing but his eyes seemed like they were urging her to trust him. "Who hurt you?"

Alex wasn't ready to tell him about the self-loathing she'd dealt with since that terrible day her sister was taken. The horrible sense of responsibility that clung to her like an iron chain. She'd never forget the overpowering perfume of lilies that blanketed the vigil, or the teardrops staining her grandmother's white blouse. *Why did you leave her outside, Alexandra?* Cold had seeped through her chest right down to her Mary Janes at her words. Alex had pushed through the crowd, curled up beneath a bush, shaking and sobbing so hard she gasped for air. No one had noticed she was gone.

No one had cared.

"This is heavy picnic table talk." Alex put both hands on the wood and shifted her legs over the bench to stand. Hank followed her closer than her own shadow and nearly tripped her. She tossed her empty bag and drink cup in a nearby trash can and out of the corner of her eye saw Jay picking up his trash from the table to follow her.

His questions had left her with an uncomfortable twinge in her stomach. For the first time since she could remember, Alex wanted to let someone in. Maybe she hesitated because her shields had been up for so long, or maybe it was because Jay had the power to get under her skin and make her feel something. Once Alex leaned on him or anyone, she was afraid she'd break. Alex had taken great care to leave feelings out of her life, as an emotional coma, so she didn't have to deal with the hurt. She wasn't sure if she'd ever be ready to come out of it.

Chapter Eight

THEY HIT STAND-STILL traffic in Washington D.C. and then again at the start of Virginia. Alex had come around a bit with each passing mile, but Jay still sensed the sadness that seemed to hover over her at lunch. She had so many different layers, and he wanted to know more about each one. He wanted to touch her despite the consequences, show her what it meant to be cared for, even if it was only physical. Could he give her anything else? All their focus should be on finding Luke, but when she looked at him under a fringe of lashes, it made his heart bump a little faster.

Outside, the world was dark except for the fast-moving sea of shiny taillights. They'd made it to the middle of the state with only a quick pit stop for coffee.

"Do you think Luke knows they're not driving to Shane's alleged ocean-facing bungalow in Florida?" He rubbed at the tension in the back of his neck.

"Depending on how fast they've traveled, they might already be at their destination. There's still a chance Fletcher was lying, but the Blue Ridge Mountains are in North Carolina. It's worth checking out. We need more info before we strap on hiking boots." Alex switched lanes to get around a slow-moving sedan and hit the gas. In the back seat Hank sprawled out and buried his face in between his paws.

"You've been at the wheel all day. Let's switch off." They could go further with two drivers, if she trusted him at the wheel.

"I don't like being in the passenger seat." Alex reached toward the center console and took a big gulp of coffee. The scents—mocha, ground coffee beans, and cream—permeated the air.

"Who does? But we can cover more ground if both of us drive. I've handled a tank, Ally." She stiffened the moment he uttered the abbreviated name, like she'd been slapped. She didn't respond. After a moment, she set down her coffee.

"No one's called me that in well over twenty years." Something in her voice had changed and the words came out in a pained rasp.

"Who?" There was a sick twist in his gut. Someone hadn't just hurt her—they'd destroyed her. Pain radiated through his jaw as he clenched his teeth. There was an uncomfortable burn in his chest when he thought of another guy mistreating her, but this was more than twenty years ago. Alex would've been a child and definitely not one old enough to have a boyfriend.

"My sister, Stephanie." Her eyes had dulled, and her straight and strong posture adopted a slight slump. "She's gone now."

"I'm sorry. I hadn't realized she'd passed." What a dumb thing to say. Of course he didn't know, because he barely knew anything about Alex, or her past. She wasn't the open-book type.

"She didn't. Well, we don't really know. That's always been the worst of it, not knowing." Her neck muscles tightened as she swallowed.

He wanted to reach out, touch her arm, whisper words of comfort, but he couldn't seem to move. After working five days a week to counsel veterans, how could he be rendered speechless? When was the last time he'd wanted to pull a woman onto his lap and just hold her? Not since his high school sweetheart Becky and look how that had turned out. He still had a hard time thinking of her, and of the wrenching betrayal.

"What happened? Do you want to tell me about it?" he asked with a soft voice, then picked up his own coffee, long cold, just for something to do with his hands.

"I don't talk about it," she mumbled and cut the wheel to dart into the deserted right lane.

"Okay. Is Lex safe?" He asked to transition them out of the uncomfortable topic.

"Two syllables too much for you?" A smile ghosted her lips, and his soul sighed with relief. It was easier, safer to keep things light and uncomplicated.

"Jay and Lex sound more like a crime-fighting team." He rested his head against the back of the seat and took another long sip of cold coffee.

"Oh yeah? What about Sam and Frodo? A perfect example of an unstoppable one-syllable, two-syllable team." Alex turned her directional on and took the next exit.

"I think I just fell madly in love with you," he said as Alex pulled into the parking lot of a closed-down dry-cleaning business. Her eyes widened and a flush crept across her cheeks.

They switched places. Jay got behind the steering wheel, adjusted the seat and mirrors to work with his much larger frame, and got back on the highway. Alex had passed him some of the control, which meant part of her trusted him. It shouldn't give him so much satisfaction, but it did. She was like a wolf who had just accepted him as part of her pack.

They drove deeper into Virginia, and it was nearly ten before they decided to pull off the highway. A blue and pink electric sign for the Whistling Duck Motel glowed through the dark and promised refrigerated air and budget prices. Adjacent to the two-story motel was a questionable-looking bar and grill.

"This okay?" Jay asked and chose a parking spot next to the front office.

"As good as any," Alex said and twisted slightly to unbuckle her seat belt. He couldn't help but notice how it sat perfectly centered in between her rounded breasts. He looked away and slid out of the car to get Hank, who had snoozed through the drive like a professional sleeper. Their trio came together at the front of the rental car. Despite the motel's odd appearance, the lot was packed. A bell chimed when Jay pushed open the glass, and the thick scent of patchouli made his eyes water. A teenage boy with shoulder-length sun-bleached hair and a hemp necklace greeted them with a goofy grin. "Welcome to the Whistling Duck, guys." The kid looked stoned out of his mind. "Whoa, I have never, ever, seen a dog that big. It's like, a horse or something."

Hank tilted his head at the compliment, then sneezed a few times and sent a string of drool flying onto the front desk. Jay located the source of the smell. White smoke drifted into the air from a dragon-shaped incense burner.

"Thanks," Jay said and pulled out his wallet. He paused and looked over his shoulder at Alex. "Two rooms, or one?"

"Do one. We don't need to waste the cash on two." Alex took a tissue out of her bag and wiped the slobber off the desk, then used a fresh one to wipe Hank's face.

"Right on." The goofy kid winked, and Jay struggled to keep his eyes from rolling.

He paid for the room, got a set of keys, and started to walk around the building with Alex.

He laid a hand on Hank's head as they sought out their room. "I think this guy got a contact high from our friend Cheech in there." The dog's tongue lapped his palm, and Alex's laugh burst into the starless sky.

They found their room, set down their bags, and got Hank his dinner and a treat. Jay had expected worse than the tired floral carpet and pineapple comforters, but it was clean and that was all that really mattered at the moment. Alex dug into her bag, pulled out the stuffed bunny and a few other toys, and arranged them on one of the double beds. His lips involuntarily lifted into a smile. He really liked her rough edges that softened out for the dog. He really liked everything about Alex.

Hank hopped on the bed, circled around a few times, and settled down with the stuffed bunny between his paws. She leaned over to give Hank a kiss on the head and her T-shirt rode up on her hips. There was a black raven tattooed on her ivory skin. He couldn't quite make out the words scrolled below it. His mouth went dry, like he'd swallowed a fistful of salt. She turned, a tidy little package of subtle curves and strength, and he forgot to breathe.

"Are you feeling brave?" Alex said with one hand on the curve of her hip.

Jay ignored the pull that traveled from chest to pelvis. "Let me guess," he said plastering on a smile. "You're hungry enough to see if the bar food will make your stomach bleed."

"I was more concerned about you." Alex smirked and went to the door. "My stomach is ironclad." She patted her flat belly and swung open the door. "We'll be back soon, Hank."

"I'll hold your hair back." He bumped her shoulder with his as they walked across the parking lot to the bar. Another laugh bubbled out of Alex. It was a pretty good sound. For one second, then two, they grinned stupidly at each other. A warmth spread through Jay's chest and traveled right down to his toes. This easy camaraderie tied up with sexual tension was an unusual feeling for him. She made him laugh so easily one moment and then turned his muscles to liquid the next. Everything about her was attractive to him from the sway of her hips to the freckles that skimmed over the bridge of her nose.

"Let's hope that doesn't happen," Alex said as they approached the flat brick building that looked almost deserted. The moment Jay opened the door, the smell of stale beer and peanuts smacked him in the face. He walked in first to survey the crowd. It looked like a rough and tumble place. It was silly to be protective of Alex when there was no doubt she could handle herself, but he was all the same. A few bikers in their leathers sat at a dimly lit corner table, and a few weathered-looking men lined the bar. The wood floors were sticky with the residue of spilled drinks and Jay's sneakers clung to them with every step. Alex and Jay chose two seats at the end of the bar and waited a few moments before being acknowledged.

"What'll it be?" the bartender said when he finally broke off his conversation with the regulars and meandered their way. He was middle-aged and wore a scowl framed by a wispy copper and gray goatee. They both ordered bottled beers. The man retrieved them, popped the tops, and slapped them down on the maple countertop.

"Godspeed." Jay tilted his bottle and handed Alex a worn bar menu that was propped up against a napkin dispenser.

"Is the layer of dust a bad sign?" she whispered and brushed a finger over the back of the menu, then on her jeans.

"As bad as the layer of grime on the floor. Unfortunately, we didn't see another option for miles, so it's this or the vending machine near the front office." Jay leaned closer as they both scanned the single menu. The sweet, fruity scent of her hair momentarily masked the bar's less than appealing smells. Her knee brushed against his as she swiveled her barstool to give him a better look at the menu and his stomach tightened in response.

"What are you getting?" Alex looked up at him and his fingers itched to tuck her hair behind her ear.

"Grilled cheese. Virtually impossible to screw up," Jay told her before the bartender walked back to their side of the bar. They ordered food and another round of drinks. Jay wouldn't have ordered chicken from this place, but he didn't have the heart to tell that to Alex who'd gotten a buffalo chicken sandwich. It didn't take long for the food to come and they both eyed their plates suspiciously and exchanged glances. Surprisingly, it looked perfectly normal.

Jay held his beer up to hers. "To ironclad stomachs." Alex chuckled and like a switch turning on a light, he grinned.

"Cheers," she said and clinked her bottle against his. Jay

drank some beer and tried his sandwich. It was mediocre at best but he'd had much worse. "Did your mom answer your texts about Amy?" Alex asked and took a bite of her own sandwich.

"Yeah, she's doing okay. She called that lady at the crisis center, Julia. Still blames herself for everything that's happened." Every time he thought of what Shane had done to her, a pounding banged in his ears, deafening, like a train roaring by inches from his face. A weird look swam in Alex's eyes, but it was gone so fast he might've imagined it. "When I came home from Afghanistan, Amy was right there during my recovery. It made us even closer than we were before. I know my other sister Courtney will be taking good care of her."

"Family can be a nice thing." Alex polished off her sandwich and pushed back the plate. Jay caught the longing in her voice. What had broken Alex away from her parents? If he'd lost a child, he'd damn well hold on to the other one as tight as he could.

"We have our moments but I wouldn't change it for a thing. Most gatherings end with us all eating way too much, because the only one in the family who can cook is my mother. Culinary skills aren't a trait she passed down to me and the girls, but I can work miracles with a microwave or telephone. What about you and your family?" Jay dropped his paper napkin over his empty plate. The bartender came over and cleared away the dishes. It was the perfect opportunity for Alex to cop out of the conversation.

"This one's on me." Alex dropped two twenties on the table, drained what was left in her bottle, and slid down from the stool. They made their way to the exit and Jay took a big gulp of the fresh air. Light from the motel sign illuminated their path, and he was uncomfortably aware of Alex next to him. The shape of her body, the smell of her skin, even the way her lips tasted were all etched into his memory and for some reason, his mind refused to let him forget. It was going to be a long night on his side of the small room.

At the door, Alex reached into her purse and fumbled the key. It dropped soundlessly before clattering against the pavement. Jay crouched down to pick it up and when he stood, he was only inches from her. She was staring at him and Jay's palm dampened against the key. He clenched the metal between his fingers quickly, then relaxed them and slid the key into the lock.

"Jay." Alex's fingers skimmed over his before he had a chance to turn the knob. He looked down at her flushed skin and was keenly aware of his heart knocking against his ribs. She stepped closer, lips parting. All he had to do was lean down to kiss her. He licked his lips and skimmed his thumb over her jawline. Jay bent toward her, and Alex rose up on her tippy toes to meet him halfway. Their lips brushed and he was drowned with warmth. There was heat beneath the sweetness of the gentle kiss and when she dipped her tongue playfully into his mouth, he wrapped an arm around the small of her back and pulled her flush against him.

The small murmur of pleasure was all he needed to deepen the kiss. Jay turned the key in the lock and pushed open the door. Alex smoothed her hands up his chest and wound her arms around the back of his neck. His pelvis tensed as she pushed her hips against him and a shock of energy speared straight to his toes. This is why he couldn't forget Alex. Every touch, every kiss, every taste brought him to the brink of madness. She made him forget everything—the explosion of shells, the screams of his enemies and friends, the smell of his own burning flesh as his ears rang and dripped blood. Jay pulled her into the hotel room and kicked the door shut with his foot. Alex made him feel drunk—a little fuzzy around the edges and empowered with confidence. The kiss in her car had left him so unsteady, he didn't take it further, but this time, if she was willing, he wouldn't pull away.

Chapter Nine

Alex stood in the center of the well-worn motel room with her arms tangled around Jay's neck. She couldn't catch her breath. She couldn't think. What the hell had she started? In the background she heard Hank's snoring and country music playing in the adjacent room. She breathed in Jay's shower-fresh scent; it was cleansing, like mist over the sea.

The primal urge to touch him had overtaken her outside and once their lips met, need had exploded in her. There was nothing worse than being vulnerable and the weird feelings swirling inside her were too needy, too dangerous.

"God, Alex," Jay said and nuzzled against her ear. "You're so beautiful." When he took her earlobe between his lips, she shuddered and began to run her hands up his shirt against his hard skin. Her fingers brushed against the first ridge of his scars, reminding her how brave and strong he was. She was about to ignore the warning bells in her mind that told her to stop being a fool and push him down on the bed when an ache spread through her stomach. Alex put her hand on Jay's chest and broke the kiss.

"What is it?" His brows creased together. A sickly sweet tingle rose up in Alex's throat and she pressed a hand to her belly.

"I just…I feel sick." Alex skirted around him and ran to the bathroom. Mortified, she hunched over the toilet and threw up. She gagged and gasped for breath before the next wave of nausea hit. Alex didn't hear Jay approach but two sturdy hands pulled back her hair as she was sick again. When the worst seemed to be over she sat back on her heels and took a few deep breaths. Her stomach was churning so badly she didn't protest when Jay rubbed her back in circular motions. The physical contact surfaced emotions that made her want to crumble.

It had been so long since someone had taken care of her. Decades. When she was a kid and got sick, she didn't inconvenience her parents. Not that they'd offered any compassion. It was clear they blamed Alex for Stephanie's disappearance, just as she did. It had hurt though, not to have someone to confide in when she'd had a bad day at school or was missing her sister. Alex even got her first period and dealt with it on her own. She'd walked to the corner store on the way home from school and bought a box of pads, praying no one would see her. At night, when everyone was asleep, Alex had turned her face into her pillow and sobbed. She'd been so lonely, but she'd come out stronger for it.

"Come on, honey," Jay said softly, still stroking her back.

How long had they been sitting there on the bathroom floor? It could have been minutes or hours—she wasn't sure. The rhythmic motion of his solid hands had lulled her into a trance. This was a completely new side of Jay, and a side of her that she preferred to keep locked away. Suddenly the careless, easy banter of the trip was replaced by something else entirely. Jay was displaying an incredibly tender side, while she was being weak. Vulnerable. Not in control.

Jay wrapped one arm around her waist and tucked the other right under her bottom and stood up, cradling her like a child.

"You don't have to carry me. I'm fine. Really." Heat spread over Alex's cheeks. Jay had just witnessed her upchucking all over the bathroom. Ugh, so much for the strong stomach she'd bragged about. "Really, at least let me brush my teeth and wash my face first."

"Okay." Jay gave her some privacy and waited outside the door, but when she came out he scooped her up all the same. Still holding her tight against him, Jay pulled down the covers and placed Alex gently on the bed. "I'll be back in just a second." He tucked the covers around her, took the room key off the nightstand, and strode to the door. Once Jay was outside, Alex placed her hand on her forehead. She'd literally flushed their intimate moment right down the drain. She'd craved the heat of his hands on her, the power that pulsed from his hardened muscles. And now, there was definitely no chance of that.

Within minutes Jay was back, carrying bottles of water and ginger ale. There was a burning behind her eyelids as he unwrapped a plastic cup from the vanity and ran water over a face towel. He approached the bed and put the cup of ginger ale on the nightstand. He squatted down next to the bed, so they were eye level. Her scalp tingled as Jay brushed the hair away from her face and gently wiped her cheeks and lips with the warm cloth. Alex was rarely speechless, but she couldn't think of one coherent thought. After he threw the towel in the sink, Jay handed her the ginger ale and sat on the end of the bed. He waited for her to take a few sips before speaking.

"Better?" His hand rested on the covers over her legs. All she could do was nod in response. The soft drink had done little to ease the lump in her throat. "So much for that ironclad stomach." Jay offered up a small grin and Alex laughed weakly.

"It's too fast to get food poisoning, but something didn't sit right," Alex said looking down into her cup. "Sorry you had to see that." She winced. Her ears and cheeks were impossibly hot and most likely as red as a lobster. Part of her was thankful it had stopped them from going further; the other more primal part was disappointed.

"It still wasn't as gross as Hank's spit flying across the motel desk." The dimple on his left cheek flashed as he smiled.

Something shifted and stirred inside her chest. Shit. He was wearing her careful defenses down. Alex watched as Jay kicked off his shoes and then scooted up to the headboard, so he was sitting beside her. His fingertips pressed lightly on her shoulders as he pulled her close, so her back was pressed against his chest.

"I'm really okay now," Alex said as her muscles tensed. A quick roll in the sheets was one thing, but this was different. Too emotionally charged and caring. She definitely didn't do intimacy.

"Let me hold you for a little. Just relax, Alex." He stroked her hair from her forehead like she was something to be treasured. "You're not used to being cared for, are you?" There was a pang of sadness in Jay's tone that touched the hollow, empty space in her heart.

"Everyone has different ways of dealing with pain," Alex said quietly and then she did something that she hadn't done since meeting Lindsey in college. She made a conscious decision to confide in him. "This afternoon, I mentioned my little sister. She was abducted from our front yard. She was only five years old. After Stephanie was taken, we were all so broken. My father holed up in his office and did nothing but work. My mother said she was putting in long hours until she confessed she was having an affair. I wasn't supposed to overhear the conversation, but I had become invisible."

Alex shivered a little and Jay pulled her closer and rubbed his hands up and down her arms.

"I'm used to taking care of myself. It's a hard habit to break. I've honestly never even had a real relationship before." She hadn't meant to say that much, but around Jay she relaxed and words seemed to slide off her tongue. Alex was stripped bare but she still couldn't bring herself to tell him what really happened that day. Even so, everything had changed.

Jay kneaded her shoulders and she melted slowly against him. "I'm sorry that was your childhood. You deserved to be cared for." His breath tickled her cheek as he spoke. A sarcastic laugh, full of self-depreciation slipped through her lips before she could stop it, but he countered it. "Whoever made you feel like you weren't enough was wrong. Dead wrong."

The strength and conviction in his voice had her actually believing it for a moment. Until she remembered that her negligence had possibly caused her sister to die at the hands of monsters. They sat in silence for a few minutes as Jay continued to massage her shoulders and rub her back. It was far too cozy, but she couldn't bring herself to shrug him away.

"What are the words tattooed on your back?" he asked softly.

"With pain comes strength." Silence hung in the air for a few moments. "I don't let people get close, Jay. I'm not sure what's happening between us, but I'm not one to be vulnerable. I'd be the worst in a relationship."

"When I enlisted, I had someone waiting for me back home. Her name was Becky." Jay's low voice cut through the quiet, its only competition the light hum of the heat coming through the vents. There was a pang in Alex's stomach, one that had nothing to do with her earlier illness. Jay was about to trust her with something, which only opened them both up for more hurt. "High school sweethearts. She was *the one*. We were inseparable before I left for my first tour in Afghanistan, then the second and third. There was nothing that could break us. Until I returned home injured. I didn't come home with the face I left with. It was a shock to her. How could it not be?"

The beat of his heart drummed against her back as the rise and fall of his chest rocked her back and forth. Jay shifted a little and started to speak again. "Still, I thought she was stronger. That a superficial injury wouldn't stand in the way of our future and the family we'd dreamed of having. I went over to my best friend's house one night after Becky stood me up for dinner. We'd known each other since diapers, and I never knocked. His house was mine and all that. So, yeah, I walked in and found my best friend and my girl having sex on the living room couch. Never even told my sisters what happened. And that's why I don't do relationships, either." Jay let out a long, ragged breath. He'd entrusted her with a devastating secret. It should have made her scared as hell. Instead, she felt important and trusted. Was she worthy of it?

"She didn't deserve you." Alex's tone was hard as fire rolled inside her chest. How could this woman make him feel like less when he returned home injured?

"I don't know about that. I'm an ugly son of a bitch," he said, laughing it off. He wasn't the type to be insecure about his scars—he was too practical for that—but the comment bothered her all the same.

"No." Alex turned her body, so she was kneeling with one leg straddled in between his legs and the other on his outer thigh. "You're seriously built, Jay. The best kind of man candy." Alex smiled when a laugh erupted from him. Her heart swelled. When was the last time she made someone feel good about themselves? "But it's not just your body." Alex leaned closer into the warmth of his hard chest and laid feather-light kisses on his smooth left cheek and the jagged ridges of his right cheek. "It's your face. Your quick smile. The scars, too. They're part of the package and, Jay…" Alex paused and whispered in his ear. "It's one hell of a package. All male, rugged and strong." She leaned back to meet his eyes and sent him a saucy smile. "Added to that, those scars make you look like you could dole out one heck of an ass-kicking. That's sexy." Alex wasn't bullshitting him. All those things made Jay so appealing to her. Then he did the unexpected and cupped her face with his rough hands and kissed the tip of her nose. He wrapped his arms around her, pulled her close, and just held on.

"My inflated ego thanks you." Jay pressed his lips to her temple.

"Oh, that's your ego?" Alex said, and shifted her eyes to the zipper of his pants.

They both laughed. "If you didn't already figure it out, I'm attracted to you. Incredibly so, but I can't offer anything more than the physical. I don't think I could if I tried."

"Me neither." Alex laughed. "Look at us, two emotional hermits talking about feelings. Might be scarier than the throw up."

"Yeah, and speaking of—you and that ironclad stomach need rest." Jay fluffed her pillows and moved the covers around her. "Sleep tight. Don't let the bed bugs bite," he said softly before kissing her forehead.

"That's not something to joke about in a place like this," Alex said, feigning seriousness. When she turned toward the wall though, she smiled through the darkness. Her mattress dipped when Hank jumped up on her bed and snuggled beside her. She lay still for a while listening to Jay's breathing deepen. Exchanging secrets with Jay made Alex's heart ache. She'd become so cold, so hard. Part of that was the lack of love and affection. First, as a child and then as an adult as she'd become more reclusive.

For the first time, though, it dawned on her that she hadn't cared for anyone either in a very long time. Whether it was selfishness or self-preservation she wasn't sure, but tonight, when she'd responded to Jay's story with kind words, a tenderness opened in her heart. Maybe keeping a protective barrier around her emotions was overrated. Or maybe letting it down would be foolish. Only time would tell.

Chapter Ten

JAY YANKED UP the zipper on his sweatshirt as he left the front office and stepped into the chilled air. It was five in the morning and everything was quiet and still at the Whistling Duck. He couldn't shake the feeling that something had changed in him. In an effort to distract Alex from her past hurts, because God they were awful, he'd shared a piece of himself with her.

It had been four years since Becky slept with Max. Four years before he told anyone that the two closest people in his world turned their backs on him when he needed them most. Like Alex, he didn't like to be vulnerable. Sharing his feelings, confiding in someone, usually made him feel like a crab without a shell—exposed and susceptible to being crushed. When he told Alex though, the opposite happened. Tension that had been tightly knotted within him had released. He wasn't angry with them anymore, either of them, he realized. Telling someone had helped him move on, healed the salt-on-skinned-flesh feel. What he didn't tell her was he'd had a ring in his pocket the night Becky stood him up. Now he was glad he'd found them together before getting into a marriage with someone who would betray him. He'd dodged a bullet there and had thrown the ring into the sea.

Sure, he helped people in the day to day, even liked most people he met, but the relationships were usually skin deep. Alex was seeping through the layers, undoing each strategically placed lock used to keep someone out and avoid more pain. Last night, they'd both trusted each other.

When he rubbed her back after she'd been sick, and she looked up at him with a bewildered stare—as if no one had ever tended or cared for her—everything inside him ached to gather her close. It wasn't a terrible feeling to soothe her, and the urge to patch up her invisible wounds scared the shit out of him at the same time.

He paused when he saw Alex coming out of the motel room up ahead. "Hey," she shouted and jogged toward him with a duffel on each shoulder and Hank loping behind. Each time his paws connected with the pavement his heavy jowls swung to the side. Once she reached Jay, she was breathless, and her eyes were bright. "I just got off the phone with Gabe. There was a theft last night at an outdoor supply store in South Carolina. He emailed the owner and got a response with a photo back." Alex held up her phone. The black-and-white security camera image depicted a skinny man with shaved blond hair and a neck tattoo.

"That's him." Jay tensed up, neck and shoulders stiffening.

She leaned in close and swiped her finger over the screen. "This is the front of the building."

A rusted four-door sedan faced the shop door head-on. His eyes narrowed, as he looked it over closely. "Hard to see, but it looks like a person in the passenger side. It could be Luke." He clamped down on the angry energy firing off inside him, making his nerves snap and his brain urge him to go, to find his nephew.

"The outline looks very similar to the pictures I've seen." Alex took her phone and tucked it in her back pocket. "I've let the police department know, so they can get on it, because we're still six hours out at best. I've packed everything from the room, so let's hit the road."

In the car, they buckled their seat belts. "Fletcher was close. It's possible they went into the woods near the store." Alex turned up the volume on the radio and Led Zeppelin singing "Ramble On" filled the car.

"Does the store owner know we're going to follow them?" Jay looked out the window. Scenery rolled by but he couldn't appreciate the vibrant green hues of sprawling farmland. All he could focus on was Luke. He was only in the next state, but it still was several hours away. His skin crawled like earthworms emerging from the dirt after a summer shower.

"Yes, and he's offered up discounted camping supplies for the search. If we decide they most likely took to the woods, we track them." Alex hit the gas and merged into the left lane to pass a slow-moving car. Jay fought the urge to grab the oh-shit handle at the top of the doorframe.

"You look a little scared there." Alex chuckled at his expression of terror.

"I've ridden in every assault vehicle you can image, but my word, woman, you have a lead foot." He said it with a smile on his face, but he meant every word. She drove like a bat out of hell. Alex's full-bodied laugh filled the car and warmth crashed over him like a wave.

"No one's told me that before." Alex cast him a sidelong look and Jay's heart forgot to beat.

"That's because Hank can't talk." Jay grinned.

It was almost ten o'clock when they neared the end of their drive through North Carolina. They'd made a quick stop for coffee and bagels midway through, but Alex more than made up the time when they got back on the road.

"The store's located in Travelers Rest. We're almost there." Alex lifted her hand as they passed the *Entering South Carolina* sign and gave him a high five, a little tradition they'd adopted each time they hit a new state. His fingers tingled where her smooth hand met his rough one. To keep himself busy, he dug out a bag of chips they'd bought at the last rest area and tore open the bag. He tilted it toward Alex first. "Want to test that stomach on something more than a dry bagel?"

"Back to being ironclad." She dug her hand into the bag. "I'm starving." Alex shoved a few chips in her mouth and chewed. "Still can't believe you held my hair back." Alex scrunched up her face in a disgusted look and Jay laughed out loud.

"I told you I would, didn't I?" He'd do it again in a heartbeat. In fact, he got closer to really knowing Alex last night than he ever had before. He liked her more with each passing second, throw up or not.

"Well, I didn't expect to get sick. I would've kicked you out of the room if I had." Alex slammed the heel of her hand on the horn as a truck swerved in front of them onto I-20 toward Columbia.

Jay raised an eyebrow. "And how easy do you think that would've been?"

Alex momentarily took her eyes off the road and gave him a once-over. "Not very, but I have a few tricks up my sleeve." Her lips curved into a sly smile and Jay's heart galloped. They had stopped in traffic and Alex gave him a sideways glance.

He locked eyes with her. "I bet you do." The words came out in a gritty rasp as heat gathered in his gut. "I want to get my hands on you, Lex."

"Likewise." She flipped on her left directional and took I-95 south to Florence.

He smirked at her response. Only Alex would be so frank, and he appreciated that about her. She told it like it was and didn't waste time on embellishments. Maybe that's why after four years, he'd decided to trust someone.

They spent two more hours on the road before passing a large sandstone wall welcoming them to Travelers Rest. Purple flowers and greenery surrounded the base of the stone. They passed a farmers market that was busy with patrons buying produce and crafts against the backdrop of rolling mountains. The GPS told them to turn left toward their destination, and they pulled into the lot of a white-shingled shop advertising hiking, camping and fishing gear. Colorful kayaks in blue, pink, and tie-dye were propped up against the front of the building, along with mountain bikes available for rent. A car sporting a large canoe on the roof backed out, leaving a vacant spot right up front for Alex and Jay.

"Well," Alex said as she shifted the car into park. "We made it." Her hair lifted as she unbuckled her seat belt, revealing the column of her neck and delicate collarbone. Warmth spread through his lower belly. "Let me check in the back and see what we need."

Jay followed her around the rear of the car. He opened the passenger side door, put on Hank's vest as he'd watched Alex do, and leashed him. She shot him a smile and popped the trunk. He couldn't help but stare as she leaned over to fish out her backpack, all subtle curves and hard lines. Hank nudged at his leg, then his hand, as if trying to distract him. "Sorry, man. Guess you don't want me looking at your mom like that." With that, the dog stopped pestering him and stood statue still except for a pant that made his tongue jiggle back and forth.

When they strode into the store, a man in his early sixties with a coarse white beard and a *Life is Good* T-shirt greeted them with a friendly wave. "You don't look like you're here to rent a kayak. Must be the folks from up North. I'm Ray, the old fool who got fleeced. I like to think the best of people; but, man…" He shook his head in disapproval but his eyes twinkled, like he was the only one in on some private joke.

"Like my coworker Gabe mentioned when he called, we're searching for a missing child. The photo you sent to us of the man who robbed your store helped a great deal. We've informed the local police department, and they're on the hunt too." Hank ruffled a beef jerky display with his inquisitive nose. Alex spoke his name, reminding him of his manners.

"Oh, that's all right. We don't mind sharing around here. May I?" The store owner took the package off the shelf and started to open it.

"Go right ahead." Alex cocked her hip and leaned against the front desk. Ray chuckled as Hank sucked up the jerky like a high-powered Dyson.

"Now, let's get you good people outfitted for a night under the stars. Tents, sleeping bags, supplies all on me. I don't care much about my stolen goods, but I do want to see that boy returned home, so I put together some packs for you. Figured you'd be in a hurry." He went behind the desk, leaned down, and slid two full camping packs across the desk. "Safe travels." The shop owner looked at Jay, then down at the military tattoos that were scrolled from his wrist to his elbow. "And thank you, son, for your service." He gave them a peace sign as they left the store.

"Hey, what are the odds that was the grandfather of Cheech from the Whistling Duck?" he asked as he took both packs from her hands. Her full-bodied laugh bloomed in the open air.

"You know, I think you might be on to something."

Together, the trio walked back to the parking lot. They were hot on the trail and Jay was itching to get moving. Luke's life could be endangered. He was probably cold, hungry, scared, and possibly hurt. Jay ground his teeth together and shook away the thought. They'd find Luke, and Shane would answer for the kidnapping and for abusing Amy.

"You look like you're going to throw a punch all of a sudden." Alex looked up at him from under her lashes and started the car.

"Nothing I'd like to do more." He stretched out his arms and balled his hands into tight fists.

"We have an hour of daylight left. Let's not waste it finding a motel room." Alex put the car in reverse and peeled out of the space.

"Agreed. We're both quick, and we can cover a few miles in an hour." Jay stole another glance at her, something he'd been doing far too often for his own good. When Ray sent them on their way with a friendly wave and bags stuffed with supplies, he couldn't help but notice one crucial detail. There was only one tent. So, while the only thing that should be on his mind was finding Luke unharmed, he kept thinking of how Alex's body fit snugly against his. And what kind of uncle was he, thinking of himself when Luke was missing? It had been a long time since he'd had feelings for a woman. It unsteadied him. She looked so fresh and pretty in the driver's seat, confident, strong, and completely in control.

His heart stuttered. Was the only reason why he was so attracted to Alex, because he wanted her so much physically? Maybe all of these awkward feelings twisting around inside him were merely from a long dry spell. Or maybe this was the real deal, and Alex was the woman who fit him just right. For both of them, it was the first crack at an emotionally intimate relationship in years. Each of them was scarred and had experienced their share of trauma. Would their pasts send their new relationship careening off a jagged cliff, or could they harness their mutual issues to build a bridge that would help them cross over it together?

Chapter Eleven

Alex was grateful for the additional camping supplies Ray had given them, though she couldn't help but immediately recognize that he'd only given them a two-person tent. Now, she was having a hard time keeping focus on the dirt trail in front of her. She craved Jay's touch, and couldn't stop imagining his solid, scarred body against hers. Logic was screaming at her to stay away because this was something more than just physical attraction and elemental lust.

Her stomach quivered as Jay walked in front of her on the trail. He was every bit a Marine as he stalked through the forest and every bit a gentleman as he held up loose branches that stretched across the trail so she could duck under them. It was such a problem that she was drawn to him both physically and emotionally.

As pitiful as it sounded, he'd provided her with something she'd craved all her life—someone who cared. Even when she took one step back, he took it with her. Typically, men were put off by her standoffish nature, something she'd honed to perfection to keep a fair distance from anyone. Not

Jay. It didn't seem to bother him in the slightest.

Alex jerked and drew in a quick breath when the toe of her shoe got caught under a root, propelling her forward. Jay turned as she was about to face-plant into the ground and stretched out his arms to catch her. With the way her mind was working today, it was almost like an omen. Could she forgive herself for losing her sister and let someone in? Could she trust Jay with her heart?

"You're distracted by something." His voice was a low whisper as he held her against his chest. If she told him the details about Stephanie's kidnapping, he'd be the first person besides her family who knew Alex was at fault. Would Jay turn away in disgust? She wouldn't blame him if he did.

"Yeah. Just two left feet." She started to step back, but Jay's hands stayed firmly on her hips.

"Liar," he said softly. "You're as graceful as a goddamn cat. Are you still feeling sick from last night? I should've thought of that before dragging you into the woods." Jay took his left hand off her hip and placed the back of his palm against her forehead.

"What are you doing?" she asked and instinctively flinched away. Her jaw and neck ached as a lump formed in her throat. Jay always seemed to be thinking of her and what she needed.

"Seeing if you're warm. You are pale." He looped one arm around her waist and started to scoop her up. Alex sidestepped to break away from his solid arms.

"I'm a redhead. I'm always pale." Alex swiped her hair away from her eyes. "And I'm not flushed from sickness. Ever since our hippy friend loaned us one tent, I've been thinking of what we might do in it. It's distracting and annoying." Her lips set into a frown when his eyes sharpened.

"Problem for both of us." He ran his hands down her arms, and goose bumps erupted over her skin. "We'll deal."

She nodded, skirted around him, and took the lead. The position she felt most comfortable in.

Up ahead, Hank barked, and Jay turned off the trail to follow him. "Lex, look at this," he called out.

She liked the sound of Jay's voice, though, as he abbreviated her name to a single syllable. Alex came up beside him and the top of her head barely aligned with his shoulder. She was of average height, but he still towered over her.

"How did I walk right past that?" Dried leaves crunched under her sneakers as she stepped a few feet into the forest.

"Because you're distracted," Jay said as they hovered over a sloppily built fire pit.

Alex ignored his comment and bent at the waist to touch the black mound of ash. "Cold. If this was theirs, at least we know Luke is getting fed." She shook her head and looked down at the drained soup cans that littered the ground. A ring of cigarette butts stood in the dirt like a white picket fence. They got back on the trail and walked single file for another mile before the sun dipped behind the tree line, making it difficult to move safely.

Alex unfolded her map of the area. Part of her wanted to push forward. The other part knew stumbling along in the dark was too risky. If one of them twisted an ankle, it would only set them back further. "It looks like we're half a mile away from the nearest campsite."

They trekked on. With each step she was aware of her heartbeat. It was pumping fast, and it had nothing to do with the physical exertion on the trail. If she slept with Jay, it wouldn't be black and white. Maybe she was getting ahead of herself or misreading the signs, but he was a man who would want more than just sex—and for the first time, so did Alex. Starting a relationship meant the possibility of promises, marriage, even children. All things Stephanie would never have because of her.

Did she dare tuck the past away and start living beyond a sixty-hour workweek? When was the last time she watched the sunset or let sand squish between her toes as she walked along the shore? Maybe all this time she'd been doing a disservice to Stephanie's memory by not leading a fulfilling life. Or maybe she was just trying to make herself feel better for wanting all those experiences her sister missed out on.

If only they weren't in a state forest, then they could hunker down anywhere they pleased. They paused a few times to offer Hank water and take some for themselves. By the time they made it to the campground, they were both using flashlights to illuminate the path. Alex paid the fee at a small log cabin situated along the trail, and chose a secluded spot surrounded by towering trees. She breathed in the scent of pine and earth, letting it soothe her lungs that burned with exertion.

Together, in the glow of carefully positioned flashlights, they unfolded the tent, and when his hand skimmed over hers, Alex's pulse thrummed a little harder. They stretched out the tent and working in tandem, anchored it to the ground with stakes. It was small. They were going to be practically sleeping on top of each other.

"I'd hate to see what a one-person tent looks like," Jay said and stepped back to look at their work. "This one looks sized for hobbits."

"Yeah, really small ones." Alex smirked through the dark.

"Between me and Hank, you'll be lucky to have a sliver of space," he teased, but he wasn't wrong.

"At least you don't snore as loud as Hank. That would put a real damper on things."

There was a fire pit, and they gathered a few stray branches to toss in for kindling. Alex flicked open the lighter she carried in her own supplies and held the glowing flame up to the dry wood. It caught alight and before long they had a crackling fire radiating heat and light. Hank sat a few feet away and cocked his head from side to side, enthralled by the dancing flames, completely ignoring the kibble she'd set in front of him.

"Ever go camping before?" Jay tossed her a protein bar

from one of the packs and joined her on a log positioned next to the fire.

"I let Lindsey convince me to go once in college. It was spring break, and I was planning to stay on campus. She dragged me with a group of classmates to Vermont, and we stayed in these little rustic cabins. It was so freakin' cold I thought I might die of hypothermia before the week was over." The memory made her smile.

"It's going to be cold tonight, too," Jay said. He may not have meant it suggestively, but a tingle shot down her spine. The smoky scent of the fire wrapped around the campsite and the crackling flames cast shadows over Jay's face.

"It's a good thing, because that insulated tent's going to be like a convection oven." Alex crumpled up her wrapper and stuffed it in her pocket. "What about you? Any camping outside the service?"

"Only in the backyard. My parents would build a fire and me and the girls would make s'mores. We had this scrappy little terrier who would steal the marshmallows right from the sticks." There was a lightness in Jay's voice, and her throat tightened. Those were the kinds of things she'd missed out on with Stephanie. If only she hadn't gone inside that day to get juice boxes, her life might be completely different. She'd be completely different.

"I thought I'd seen the last of dinner packaged in a wrapper when I got discharged." Jay tore the foil down and polished off the last of his bar. "Not exactly cookies and cream flavored as advertised, but then again neither were the MREs the Marines tossed to us."

"What was the easiest one to choke down?" Hank had finally eaten his dinner and settled by her side.

"Hah. Well, the safest bet was always spaghetti but it's nothing like the homemade kind—and when I say that I mean from the box with some jarred sauce." Jay rested both elbows on his knees and grinned at her.

"I buy the frozen variety more often than not. They're easier and don't make dishes." Alex pulled up the hood on her sweatshirt to stop the wind from tousling her hair.

Jay leaned his knee into hers with a friendly nudge. "When we get back you can come to my place for dinner. I'll pull out all the stops—boil water, get a jar of sauce, maybe even a garlic bread from the freezer aisle," he joked, and her laugh echoed through the night.

"I had no idea you were a hopeless romantic." Alex leaned back with her hands firmly positioned on the log, stretched out her legs, and crossed them at the ankles. The easy stance helped her to dismiss the sensations she usually ignored, like her heartbeat quickening each time he laughed or the prickle of her skin when his knee bumped her outer thigh.

"Is that what you're looking for, Alex? Romance?" At that moment, with hoot owls and the snap of burning firewood in the background, she wanted nothing more than to be folded into his arms where it was warm and safe.

Chapter Twelve

THE SECOND THE words left his lips, Jay instantly regretted them. This was a game neither of them would win.

"I'm not a flowers and chocolates type." Alex cast her eyes to the ground for a moment, then back to him. Her pupils looked impossibly large and her lips ripe and red. "But the way you took care of me when I was sick, the way you make me laugh, those things I find incredibly romantic." In a movement only Alex could make fluid and graceful, she twisted and brought one leg over his lap, so both knees rested against the outsides of his legs. Jay's pulse hummed as he looped his arms around her.

"I'm starting to feel grateful for the small tent." Even as he smiled at her, a knot twisted in his stomach. Alex wasn't bashful about sharing what was on her mind—except when it came to emotions, and now she'd just confessed to having feelings for him on an emotional level. He hadn't even come to terms with his own mess of feelings he was developing for Alex.

"I want you," she admitted, never breaking eye contact.

Jay let out the breath he'd been holding and pulled her against him. She smelled salty and sweet from the day of hiking and the lemon meringue scent she wore. Jay breathed her in and filled his lungs with cool, clean air. Screw it. He'd deal with the consequences later.

"Lex," he murmured and dropped his eyes to her full lips. They stayed inches apart for one, then two heartbeats as anticipation grew thick, like a weighted blanket circling them both, drawing them closer. When he touched his lips to hers and sank into the kiss, every cell in his body roared to life. She tasted like chocolate and vanilla, much better than the sweetened protein bar they'd consumed minutes earlier.

Alex ran her hands over his chest and down his shoulders, making his body hum with pleasure. He deepened the kiss, loving the way her tongue played against his. Jay gripped the backs of her thighs and lifted her, so Alex's legs wrapped neatly around his waist. They were as close as could be. The only barrier separating them was clothing, and the pressure of Alex against his most sensitive parts made him ache.

Jay stood up from the log, hands still firmly laced around her, lips still connected, and began walking to the tent. He placed her down when they reached it and instantly missed the feel of her against him as he unzipped the opening. Alex slid in first and lay on her back with her elbows propping her up. He kicked off his sneakers and carefully climbed in with her, positioning his body over hers.

She leaned back and skimmed her hands under his T-shirt, over his stomach and chest, sending a current of sensations rippling to his core. The fire outside gave him just enough light to see emotion reflecting in her eyes. Alex was letting him in. This wasn't just physical. Panic trickled through his chest, icy and cold. Her lips were parted and her eyes fluttered shut. She liked to be in charge, but she was handing over the reins to him now. And with that, his heart slipped and faltered. He swallowed hard and hesitated. The feelings for her swamped him all at once and he needed a moment to get his bearings.

"What is it?" Alex said and sat up slightly. Jay wasn't ready to let her know the depth of his feelings for her. Wasn't even sure if he could give her what she deserved. It had been so long since he'd cared for a woman and the onslaught of it rocked him like a tidal wave. Alex hadn't had a lot of love in her life, and Jay wanted to make sure if she trusted him with her heart, he'd be able to take care of it. Even though Alex and Becky where different in every way he could think of, he still had some hesitations about starting a relationship. Two of the closest people in his life had turned on him when he'd been struggling mentally and physically.

"Nothing." Jay rested his weight on his forearms and leaned down to kiss her, slowly pushing her back. When they found Luke and returned to their separate lives, would she be done with him? Too busy with keeping her firm running? It was already too late to turn back now, no way to reverse his feelings for her.

Alex's hands pushed against his chest and brought him back to the moment. "Stop. Just stop." She pushed out from under him and sat up straight. "Are you having second thoughts?"

"God, no. My mind just wandered for a second. Sorry." He sat up across from her, hunching to fit in the tiny space. They fell back into the kiss and in an extremely tender gesture she brought her fingertips to the sides of his face. He paused, breathing heavily. Alex wanted and accepted him in a way that Becky never did.

"What is it?" Alex asked as she pressed her lips over the rough scars on his cheek.

"I haven't done this in a long time." Even as he combed his fingers through her silky hair, she tensed up.

"You're thinking of your ex?" There was no emotion in Alex's voice and her face was unreadable.

"No," Jay said too quickly and her eyes narrowed. "Maybe, but not in the way you think." *What a dumbass.* The cold look she gave him was enough to chill the entire tent. There was something else there, too. Hurt. Jay didn't know how to make it right without digging a deeper hole.

"If you're not over her after how she treated you, I can't compete with that," Alex said dully. He was at a loss. Jay had a feeling if he told her the truth—that it wasn't Becky he was in love with at all—she wouldn't believe him right now. And if she did believe him, it'd scare her into running away for good. "We have an early morning. Hopefully, tomorrow we finish what we set out to do." Alex rolled over onto her side away from his touch.

"Hey," he said and stroked his hand down the length of her arm. "It's not what you think. I don't want you falling asleep angry."

She looked back at him with a hard stare. "There's not enough room for three of us in this tent, Jay. You're the one who invited your ex in."

Jay released a pent-up breath. There would be no getting through to her tonight. He backed out of the tent and nearly fell over Hank, who was lying at the threshold. The dog slapped his tail against the dirt a few times. "Guess you'll be the one sleeping in the tent," he muttered and moved to the side so the dog could move in. Jay zipped the tent closed once Hank climbed inside.

The fire had reduced to a low smolder but it still was giving off enough heat to chase away some of the chill in the nighttime air—the same couldn't be said for the chill in Alex's voice. He should go back in there and wake her, show her how he felt without a single word. He had never wanted to fall for someone again—yet it snuck up on him like a high tide inching toward shore. Maybe the circumstances of searching for Luke and being in confined quarters together had intensified what he was feeling.

They were the worst possible choice for each other. Both of them had difficulties with emotion; both of them had been hurt. Maybe that's exactly why they needed each other, exactly why they fit together so well. They both understood pain and loss, and perhaps together they could come to understand more of contentment and peace. But only if she was willing to let him in. After tonight, he wasn't sure she ever would.

Chapter Thirteen

Alex opened her eyes to sunlight penetrating through the material of the tent. A bead of sweat rolled down her forehead and she swiped it away with her hand. The material was designed to insulate, making it hot and stuffy. She sat up and a dull ache radiated down her lower back. Served her right for camping without the padding of a sleeping bag. Alex groaned when the events of last night came charging into her mind. For the first time, she'd opened herself up and it had backfired in the worst way.

Alex had been concerned about hurting Jay, but in the end, it had been her lying alone in the tent with an ache in her chest. She pressed the heel of her hand to her sternum. It hurt. The moment she'd asked if he was thinking about Becky, Alex had regretted it. There was no reason to jump to conclusions—but she had, and she'd been right. Jay had admitted it. What kind of fool was she to fall for someone who was in love, or at least still stuck on someone else? Alex shot upright. Was she really in love with him, or was it because someone else held his heart that her stomach was twisted up like gold chains at the bottom of a jewelry box?

Alex let out a deep breath and swallowed hard. She had never cried over a man before, but now hot tears burned in the corners of her eyes. What was wrong with her? She reached down to her feet and yanked her duffel bag onto her lap, swearing when the zipper stuck. Alex jerked at it and let out a low growl. She just wanted to find Luke and put as much distance between her and Jay as possible. Not because he'd done anything wrong—he'd been completely honest with her, but she was silly for wanting something she couldn't have, and deep down knew she didn't deserve.

Finally, the duffel gave way and she pulled out a fresh T-shirt and jeans. There was barely enough room to stretch out and Alex fought to get the shirt over her head. By the time she wiggled awkwardly into the jeans, she'd worked up a sweat. Desperate for cooler air she burst out of the tent, took a full breath, and wiped her forehead with the back of her hand.

Jay was sitting on the log with both elbows resting on his knees. He looked up and their eyes connected. Should she pretend last night never happened? Play it cool and brush it off? Jay stood up and closed the distance between them in a few powerful strides.

"Morning," he said and caressed her disheveled hair. "I have some things to say to you."

Alex shook her head. She really didn't want to hear some half-assed apology that would further embarrass her. Alex wasn't being fair but dammit, she couldn't help it. "We need to get moving." She stalked over to the tent and started pulling out stakes.

"I'm capable of talking while we pack up the tent," Jay said. His chin was set in a stubborn line.

"Please," she said holding up both hands. "Let's not do this right now." Another woman might be able to brush this off, but Alex had never felt this way before. Maybe because she'd been pushed aside by her family, she had been waiting for Jay to do the same. Or maybe she was using Becky to slam the door shut on a possible relationship with Jay because she was scared. Either way, she was afraid to hear him out. What if she made a mistake and pushed him away? Or worse, what if she fell into his arms only to get hurt later?

They left the campsite in strained silence and continued to hike, the tension between them pulling tighter with every step. Had she ever felt this boxed in while outside before? She risked a glance behind her, and Jay's face was taut, his muscles rigid. A crack sounded in the distance and Alex stopped and held a hand out for Jay to do the same. What was that sound in the distance? Voices? A bird's cry? Jay came up beside her and they waited. For a few moments only the sound of their breath could be heard.

"Fuck! Get back here, kid." The words ripped through the forest, violent and explosive. Hank's low growl sounded at her side, and his body went still as a statue waiting for her command. She looked at Jay, and together they broke into a run. There was no disguising their approach, but that didn't matter now. Their shoes slapping against the earth sounded like a herd of elephants thundering through the forest. A flash of yellow appeared on the trail in front of them, then Luke's bloodied face came into view. He was running toward them, sprinting for his life. When the boy turned on the trail he spotted them, and his expression crumpled with exhausted relief.

"Luke, hang in there, buddy," Jay whispered under his breath as they continued to run toward him. Jay drew his weapon from the holster on his hip, and clicked the safety off. They were so close to Luke, mere yards away, when Shane broke onto the trail and flattened him against the ground with his body. Before either of them could react, Shane pulled his handgun and pressed it against the boy's temple.

Jay's fingers pressed into Alex's upper arm, yanking her to a stop. "Hank, stay!" she commanded. They were so close, she could see the sweat pouring off Shane's skin. He'd been chasing Luke for a long time and was bound to be pissed off and unpredictable.

"Shane." Alex's voice was steady and cool, contrary to the dips and dives her stomach was taking. "All we want is Luke. You put that gun away, we let you leave here. All we want is Luke," she repeated.

Shane's bitter laugh broke through the trees. "You must think I'm an idiot. The second I turn you'll put a bullet in my back." Her chest tightened. Shane's eyes were wild and violent. "No, I know there's only two ways this plays out. I'll be leaving in cuffs or a body bag, so what the hell does it matter?" Shane cocked the gun and Jay sucked in a breath through his teeth and went rigid beside her.

"Tell us what you want. Anything. It's yours, no questions asked. Listen, I'm just going to move my right arm back and holster my weapon. We don't want any trouble." Very slowly Jay did as he said and secured the gun. *That's it.* He was doing all the right things, talking Shane down, making him believe they weren't a threat, something that wasn't easy for a man who towered over six feet and looked completely menacing.

"Your bitch sister will have every canine unit in the country snarling at my heels," he spat, eyes locked on Jay's face.

She tugged Hank's collar, moving him slightly behind her. The dog shook with fear, completely out of character for him, or any mastiff for that matter.

"We have money." There was a tremor in Jay's voice. He was obviously scared to death on the inside, but he remained in complete control. Any waver in his voice was being intentionally placed. Luke's eyelids were closed tightly, but his body jerked as he silently sobbed.

"How nice of you to remind me," Shane shouted. "You never let me forget it when I was a kid. Just some loser who knocked up his girlfriend. Your dad gave me a fat check to get out of Dodge, and hell yes, I took it. I had a future, man.

How could I be strapped with a kid and a family of tightwads the rest of my life?"

Good job, Jay, keep him talking. She continued to shuffle forward ever so slightly.

"Why then? Why take him now?" Jay's fists were balled tightly at his sides, but he seemed to be controlling the rage that made his arms tremble. How long could he be expected to hold it together?

"Is your skull that thick? I hate you people. You made me feel like scum, never accepted me. Your family stole my confidence and offered me too much cash to turn down. So, Imma steal something of yours, too." The finality in Shane's voice cued her next move.

She rocketed forward. Shane took the gun momentarily off Luke's temple to redirect it to her chest, and Alex used all her strength to leap forward. Her body slammed into Luke, and she covered him like a shield. A shot fired, a violent echo through the peaceful trees. Alex expected to take a bullet, and she braced for the pain. It didn't come but Shane groaned beside her.

Pounding footsteps boomed against the trail. A flash of Jay's tan boot crossed her line of sight. He bound Shane's arms and ankles with zip ties, something she didn't even know he carried. She filled her lungs with a deep, satisfied breath. Jay hadn't shot Shane, but a loose tree branch hanging above him. It had been a calculated risk, but it paid off, and now Luke didn't have to see blood pouring out of his biological father.

"You're safe now," Alex whispered to the trembling boy. The weight of Jay's muscular arms pressed into her shoulders as he encircled them both in a hard hug.

"Everything's all right now," he said as Luke's sobs broke loose and echoed through the trees.

"Think you broke my nose," Shane wailed. He tried to sit up, groaned, and fell back. Alex released her hold on Luke and moved over to Shane. His gasping, furious breaths rocked against her palm as she pressed on his collarbone to prevent him from moving again.

"You're lucky that's all that broke," Alex snapped, as Jay scooped Luke up and carried him off the trail, sitting him on the mossy ground with his back supported by a colossal rock. Alex reached into her back pocket and took out her phone to check the signal. It looked spotty at best. "We shouldn't try to move him." Alex gestured toward Shane who was still lying right where he'd fallen. "I have no cell service here. I'm going to walk around and see if I can get a connection. I won't go far." Alex began circling around the woods with her eyes trained on the bars of her phone. It took several minutes but once she found a small clearing surrounded by smaller trees, one bar turned to two, then three, then four. Alex dialed emergency services.

"Nine-one-one. This line is recorded. Where is your emergency?" The brisk voice was female.

"Blue Ridge Mountain Park. We're on the Black Rock

Falls trail about five miles from Pine Clearing campsite." There was a brief pause before the dispatcher spoke.

"I'm going to transfer you to Mountain Search and Rescue. Please stay on the line." A few beeps sounded in her ears before she was connected. Alex rattled off the same information, plus their coordinates from her cell phone. Now all they had to do was wait and hope Luke didn't have any serious injuries. Alex climbed back to the place she'd left Jay and Luke.

"I connected with a rescue team. They'll be here within the hour." She swiped a trickle of sweat away from her temple. Jay was still crouched over his nephew, supporting his neck with one hand, and holding a bottle of water to his lips with the other.

"Thank you." Jay shot her a grateful glance before turning back to Luke. "Slow down there. You don't want to drink too much, too fast." Luke slowed his frantic gulps to sips. The teen's lips were cracked and there was dirt and blood all over his face.

"I'm so sorry, Uncle Jay." Luke's shoulders bobbed up and down as another wave of tears came. "This is all my fault. I wanted to meet my dad so bad, I ignored all the warning signs. It was supposed to be just a quick visit and a ride around the block." Hank whimpered and rested his head on Luke's lap. "I can't believe how stupid I was to get into a car with someone I didn't know. When I realized he was driving away from town, I panicked, and he knocked me out. I swear I didn't know he was going to leave Chatham." Luke laid his head back against the boulder and looked up at the sky. Tears shimmered in the corners of his eyes.

Jay squeezed Luke's shoulder and a hard lump formed in her throat. He was a good man, one of the best she'd ever met. Maybe it was the overwhelming relief at finding Jay's nephew that had her turning away to blink back burning tears, or maybe it was the sense of mounting loss. Their shared journey was over, and nothing was anchoring them together. Jay still had feelings for his ex, and let's face it, under the façade of a well-organized business owner, she was an emotional train wreck. They had no business being together.

She glanced back, and Luke had his arms crossed around his waist. "It wasn't supposed to be like this." Anguish soaked his voice, and Alex had to press her shirtsleeves against the corners of her eyes. The poor kid was grieving for the father he thought he'd found, and the hopes and dreams of another parent's love, the memories they might make, and the bond they might share.

"I know it's not fair, bud." Jay sat down next to him and without saying a word put his arms around his shoulders. The simple words settled like slow-falling ash into the hollow of her heart. The open, sore place that Stephanie's disappearance had left dead and bleak. No, it certainly wasn't fair for a fatherless child to see dads cheering from the bleachers during a sporting event, only to wonder what made those parents stay while yours left. It wasn't fair for a family to experience the choking void of a missing child each time they passed the colorful birthday balloons on the neighbor's mailbox, marking another year, another milestone for their child.

The sound of four-wheelers rumbling down the trail yanked her out of the black place she rarely visited anymore. It was much better to remember sticky Popsicle fingers, summer picnics, and the breathless fun of sledding in winter with Stephanie tucked against her. She shook the melancholy off. Today was a day for celebration, not for reliving loss. A mother would be reunited with her child. That's what constantly kept her moving forward. Alex stood to the side as responders assessed Luke and took his vitals. The air filled with the static voices of multiple emergency radios mixed with the song of a small, cinnamon-breasted bird that poked out of the trees to assess the commotion.

The leaves crunched under Jay's heavy boots as he came to stand beside her.

"Lex." Emotion swamped his voice, and he moved closer, palms open to take her hands in his. When his steady eyes took ahold of hers, it was suddenly hard to breathe, like she was cemented in his gaze. The urge to run tangled with the soul-deep pull that drew her renegade feet a step closer.

"Excuse me." A man with sandy, cropped hair approached, and the moment dissolved. "We're going to take your nephew down on a stretcher as a precaution, and an ambulance will transport him to the nearest hospital. One of you can ride with him, and I'd be happy to drop someone off there."

"Thank you," Alex said. "Jay will ride with Luke and I'll take our rental car." The group of responders were gathered a few yards away, getting ready to begin the descent.

"Great. An officer will check in later to take your statements." Alex glanced down to where Shane was being formally handcuffed, head hung low. This offense would keep him locked up for a very long time, and the grim reality of the situation finally seemed to resonate.

Loaded up on four-wheelers, they made the rocky trip back to where they had entered the state park the day before. Alex could've been relaxing on a porch swing or in front of a charging bull for all she knew. Her mind was lost in the moment she'd shared with Jay, and for the first time, Alex dreamed of committing herself to something other than her PI firm. Except, he still had feelings for the woman who'd wronged him. Alex had never backed down from a fight for something she wanted, but then again, the stakes had never been so high. The stakes had never been her heart.

Chapter Fourteen

J AY SAT VIGIL as soft light filtered through the blinds, highlighting a strip of tile floor and the adjustable tray with an empty plate, a Styrofoam cup, and a half-eaten container of butterscotch pudding. The abrasions on Luke's face had been treated with antiseptic and butterfly bandages, and his light snores mingled with Hank's more jarring ones. His nephew had instantly taken to the dog. Hank might not be much of a guard dog, but he was going to be one hell of a therapy dog. Beside him, Alex sat quietly. She was in every sense of the word a hero, brave and fearless. The way she'd used her body to shield Luke was admirable, and it had scared the life out of him. Two people he cared about in the line of fire was all too familiar after his tours overseas.

He propped his elbow on the armrest next to Alex and slid his pinkie finger under hers. She curled her finger in, connecting them. Alex looked up at him under lush lashes, those beautiful eyes shining directly into him. He was completely aware of his heart bumping in an unsteady sort of rhythm. One that only she could provoke. The air stirred with the chirp of monitors, the light scent of lemon mingled with antiseptic and the snap of longing. Alex stroked her finger over the top of his, a gesture as intimate as the ones shared on the campground. Pain radiated in his chest, followed by warmth. Alex was the rolling current and he was being pulled under, deeper and deeper. He didn't fight it, but simply drowned in her golden eyes. He lifted his left hand and caressed his thumb over her cheek.

"You're amazing, Lex," he whispered quietly, not wanting to wake Luke.

"No." She shook her head. "We're amazing together." She pulled her little finger out of his and held her palm against his. Their job was done, but what had awakened between them was just beginning.

The door handle clicked and with one last gaze that spoke to the promise of things to come, they broke apart. Amy, his older sister Courtney, and his parents crept quietly into the room. He stood up and embraced each of them.

"How did you get here so fast?" He hadn't been expecting them until the next day. At the earliest midnight.

"When you texted me yesterday to let us know they'd been spotted, we caught the first flight we could," Amy said. She sucked in a breath and skirted around him to stand by the bedside.

"We couldn't let her come alone," his mother said. At just over five feet tall, he had to angle his head down to speak to her. June Hall might be petite, but she had a quiet strength. His mother peered around him and a smile bloomed on her face. Without speaking she gave Alex a hug. Her brows shot up in surprise, and she awkwardly patted June's back. Poor Alex was definitely out of her comfort zone as Courtney threw her arms around her, too. In a rare show of emotion, the sergeant hugged him, squeezed Alex's shoulder, and whispered a thank you.

When the doctor and child specialist entered the room, everyone but Amy and Hank, who was far too comfortable in his position on the floor to move, cleared into the waiting area.

"I'm going to run down to the lobby and get everyone some coffee and snacks. Alexandra, dear, will you help me carry it back?" His mother was using her sweetest tone and it horrified him. He couldn't tell if she was about to grill Alex or unload a host of embarrassing stories about him.

"Of course." Alex nodded and took a few no-nonsense steps to the elevator. Her spine straightened when his mother linked arms with her, and as the steel door closed shut, she sent him a pleading look.

"Momma bear taking care of her tough man-cub." Courtney laughed behind him. "When we walked in on the moment you guys were having, I swear I saw a spring in Mom's step."

Jay sighed and turned when his father cleared his throat. "By God, the woman's certifiable. She won't rest until she has enough grandchildren to fill a tour bus," his father said dryly from behind his newspaper. Courtney's laugh burst from her lips and she quickly slapped a hand over her mouth. If coffee was the only thing on June's agenda, she would have just sent their father down to get it.

"Do you take cream?"

"Cream, sugar, syrup, I take it all," Alex said. She helped herself to one of the self-serve cups.

Jay's mom raised a brow. "Darling, I hope you're more selective with men."

She nearly choked on a breath of air at the woman's dry sense of humor "Mrs. Hall, if there was a coffee named in honor of my love life it would most certainly be Limited Edition Light Brew. I work a sixty-hour week. Not too much time for romance." Was that disappointment that flashed in June's well-lined eyes?

Jay's mom added a splash of cream to her coffee and patted Alex's arm. "I see a nice sunny table by the window, let's go sit."

Alex fought the urge to roll her eyes up toward the ceiling. This was a hospital, not a French café. "What about everyone else?"

"Oh, we can get theirs on the way up. They'll be easier to carry if we drink ours now, don't you think?" June's syrupy smile was hiding meddling intentions; now she was sure of it. Alex weighed her options, not quite sure how to handle Jay's mother. How could she tackle missing persons cases, but one five-foot-nothing mama had her way out of her depth?

What was she still doing here anyway? The job was over and it had a fantastic outcome. She should be hitting the road to get back to her firm. Gabe was probably more than ready to have her back. She was more than ready to go back—except there was the nagging issue of Jay. Or rather, her and Jay. What happened next? Were all these feelings the result of a week-long road trip?

"I want to hear all about the woman who rescued my grandson," June said over her cup.

"I'm afraid it's a rather boring tale. I graduated college, moved to Boston and started my own PI firm. I work late most nights, then go home to my apartment with Hank and throw in a frozen dinner." Was she trying to make her life seem completely lame? Or was that the sad truth?

"Hank?" Disapproval iced over her words. Did every woman Jay encountered receive a grilling?

Alex decided to make her sweat it out. She leaned back in her chair and took a long sip from her cup. Heat, warm and sweet, trailed down her throat. "He's a true gentleman. Tall, dark, and handsome, too." June's mouth set in a frown and a crease appeared on her forehead, but for the first time since they'd come downstairs Alex was enjoying herself. "He loves to go for runs with me, which is pretty vital due to my sugar consumption." She held up her coffee cup and smiled.

"Where did you meet?" June asked and glanced out the

window, disinterested.

"Mastiff Rescue League of Boston." Alex took another sip of her coffee and June's eyes snapped back to attention. She laughed and spread her right hand over her chest, eyes twinkling at Alex. "I think you're trying to beat me at my own game." June tilted her head to the left and smiled. It seemed they were sharing a moment of humor, like they had made a small connection.

"I'm so glad you were only trying to fool an old woman. I was so disappointed. I hoped that maybe you were seeing my son—who is also a true gentleman and a decorated hero at that."

Alex sat up a little straighter. Jay hadn't shared much with her about his scars, only the basics, and she wasn't one to pry. If someone wanted you to know something, they'd tell you.

"He's been nothing but a gentleman on this trip." He'd comforted her when she was sick, slept outside their tent after they'd had an argument, and made her pulse gallop beneath her skin while never pushing her into something they weren't ready for. Alex wet her lips, then added, "We haven't spoken much about his time in the military."

June's chin lifted a few inches and she flipped her hair back. "Well, Jay's always been modest. The reason he has those scars is because he saved three fellow Marines when their convoy hit an IED. He pulled the passenger from his vehicle and ran back into the flames for two more. He received a purple heart for valor."

"That doesn't surprise me at all. You must be very proud."

"Oh, of course. I just wish he'd meet a nice girl. He was with his high school sweetheart for a long time but when he came back, he broke it off." She clicked her tongue against her cheek and shook her head. "Such a shame."

"If he did, I'm sure she wasn't deserving of him. He doesn't seem the type to take decisions lightly."

June took her statement as an opportunity to ramble on about every achievement Jay had ever made from his first lost tooth to the day he received his driver's license. Alex tapped her foot against the table and turned her empty cup in a clockwise motion. Several times she glanced around the room for a clock and couldn't find one. Why didn't she wear a watch? Her cell phone was in her purse, which was hanging on the chair behind them. When June stopped to take a breath before jumping into the next tale, Alex couldn't wait any longer.

"Maybe we should take the others their coffee?" Alex shimmied out of her seat and let out a breath. It wasn't that she didn't care about all of Jay's accomplishments, but she'd rather be upstairs with him than hear about him. Plus, Hank was still in Luke's room, and though he'd had his first round of formal therapy training, he was still green. They poured coffee and picked up bagels before taking a quiet elevator ride back to the fourth floor. When the elevator door opened, she couldn't burst out fast enough. Her muscles were limp with relief. She'd never had to endure a mama-grilling before. She wondered if she was as intimidating as a PI as Jay's sweet little mother was over a cup of hospital coffee.

Jay glanced up from a magazine, met her eyes, and offered an apologetic grimace. She chose the chair next to him and he leaned in to whisper in her ear. "Apologies for any horrors my mother shared with you." His breath tickled her ear and she fought the urge to lean in to him. "The police were up while you were getting coffee. I shared a statement, but they'll want yours too. They're in with Luke now."

Thirty minutes later, she'd told the police officer her take on the chain of events. When law enforcement left, Jay straightened. "We need to get some rest, but we'll be back to say goodbye before we head home."

The acidic coffee churned in her stomach. This would be the first time Jay and Alex were alone together now that their job was done. Would the lack of a common goal change things? So much had been left unsaid after she kicked Jay out of the tent last night. It was only a matter of time before he brought it up again, and she wasn't sure she wanted to unleash the microburst of emotions twisting around inside her. Ones that weren't safe to feel when Jay's heart was still stuck on his high school sweetheart.

"We'll just get Hank and say goodbye to Luke," Alex announced. Jay stood up and grasped her hand as June looked on, eyes widening. In the hospital room, Hank greeted her with a slobbery kiss. Luke's breathing was slow and deep and they chose not to wake him. After saying final goodbyes, they got into the rental car and stopped at the first hotel they could find. Alex's nerve endings stirred and snapped with electricity as Jay laced their fingers together, slowly and deliberately. At the hotel, Jay asked for one room and Alex pretended to be preoccupied with something on her cell phone.

Wordlessly, they took the elevator to the third floor, and Jay swiped one of the plastic key cards at the door. Alex tossed her duffel down and popped open Hank's portable dishes, filling one with water and the other with kibble. Instead of eating, Hank staked his claim on the pullout couch where he circled and lay down. When she turned around, Jay was right behind her.

"I'm not letting you off that easy." The gruffness in his tone chased a tingle down her spine. "What happened with Becky hurt, and the decision she and my best friend made to sleep together took a long time to move past. But it's over now, Lex. And if I was thinking about her last night, it was being thankful that it was all in the past. That's all."

Her stomach quivered when he took a step toward her, then another, until the cool wallpaper was pressed against her back. She looked up at his face, both intimidating and sexy, and the look in his eyes made her blood heat as it pumped through her veins. She started to speak but he didn't wait to hear, instead Jay braced his hands on either side of her head and crashed his lips down on hers. She had to stifle a moan when Jay slid his tongue over hers and fisted his hands in her hair.

"You, Lex. You're the only one I want." He pulled her back only long enough to look her dead in the eyes before plundering back into the kiss. It was clear what he wanted when his hips were molded against hers. Throwing her earlier anger and hurt aside, she moved her hands over his lean hips as he left urgent kisses along her jawline and neck.

She gasped when he sucked on her breast through the thin T-shirt before dragging it over her head. Clothes disappeared one by one and landed in a pile on the floor. Jay cupped her bottom and boosted her up so her legs were wrapped tightly around him. Each touch was more demanding, more possessive, and she moved with him beat for beat until her earlier doubts were buried under a swell of pleasure.

Chapter Fifteen

Jay woke with Alex in his arms and Hank at his feet. He relished the quiet moment, pleased beyond measure she hadn't slipped out of bed before him. He snuggled her a little closer and enjoyed the warmth of her body and the scent of her hair. She was strong, soft, and sweet all at the same time. Had he ever been this content?

Last night hadn't gone as planned, but the moment hadn't seemed right for the words he'd rehearsed in his head. Her actions yesterday had left him in awe of her as a private investigator and as a woman. Alex had risked everything for his nephew, and for his family. Warmth tingled down his torso as she stretched against him and flipped on her side.

"Morning." He pushed a lock of Alex's hair out of her face, and even mussed from sleep it slipped through his fingers like silk. Sunlight fought through the gaps in the blinds and illuminated each strand, saturating the red and gold colors.

"Morning," Alex said softly. He licked his lips when her hands stroked up his chest. She'd become so important to him in such a short period of time, yet he had no idea if she felt the same emotional connection. Alex touched her lips to the bottom of his chin and he looked down into her eager eyes. Yes, she wanted him on a primal level, but her wretched childhood had left a crack in her soul. Could he be the man to mend it? He drew her closer into an unhurried kiss. When she eased back it was like starting to wake from a dream and grasping at the threads of it.

"Thank you, Lex, for what you did yesterday." They lay on their sides, hips aligned, and eyes fastened together in a steady gaze. He caressed her cheek and pressed a kiss to her forehead. His heart was full and satisfied, like leaning back on his parents' oversized couch after Thanksgiving dinner. "I can't repay you. Not in this lifetime." Jay shook his head. "Not in a thousand lifetimes."

A light, rosy blush crept up her cheeks. "I only did my job."

"Yes, because to you shielding a thirteen-year-old boy who you've never met is just an ordinary day at the office." When she averted her eyes to his chest, he cupped her chin and brought her gaze back to eye level. "Lex, do you know why you think that way?" he whispered.

She swallowed and shook her head. This woman, who remained cool and collected inches from the barrel of a loaded pistol, shied away from any form of praise or appreciation. "It's because you're not ordinary. The way you live your life for others, the way you think, and the way you conduct yourself are all extraordinary. You, Alexandra

Macintyre, are extraordinary."

He was silent, letting the words resonate. Her sharp eyes softened, and for a moment they developed a glassy sheen, which she quickly blinked away. Alex slipped back and sat on the side of the bed. He knew she'd disagree, but he thought of all she'd been through and knew what he'd said was true. Her sister had been taken, her family life had been a complete cluster, but she'd made something of herself all the same—*helped people.*

"You think I'm all those things." Alex's voice cracked. "I'm not."

Jay swung his legs over the side of the bed. His bare feet sank into the plush carpet as he rounded the bed and then he knelt down in front of Alex.

"Tell me why you don't think so," he said and looked up at her.

Alex pinned her arms across her stomach, like what she was about to tell him made her physically ill. There was a twinge in his own gut as he waited for her to speak; the only sound was the occasional roll of bell cart wheels outside the door and Hank's steady snores.

"Whatever pain Stephanie faced at the hands of her abductors was my fault." She clenched her hands into constricted balls, released them, and tightened them again.

"You were just a child, Lex." He tucked his hands behind her calves and rubbed up and down the length of her legs.

"I didn't tell you the whole story," she mumbled, not

meeting his gaze.

"Tell me. Help me understand why you feel so responsible." On the floor beside the bed, Hank stretched out to an impressive length and then rolled back into a snoring ball.

Alex drew in a long, pained breath. "It was summertime, and my parents asked me to watch Steph. We were playing outside, coloring on the driveway with chalk. It was August, and you could practically see the heat rising up from the roadway. I ran inside to get us juice boxes. I left her alone in our driveway." Her voice was raw and she slapped away a tear, like a mosquito had landed on her cheek. "When I came out, she was standing beside a white commercial van. The passenger side door was ajar, and a man with a baseball cap looked up at me. The moment I looked him in the eyes was the first time I felt true fear. I knew what he was about to do. I screamed for her to come back to me, and the man grabbed her by the wrist and pulled her in. I chased the van until it disappeared, wasting time when I should've called the police." Her chin quivered, and she swiped the heel of her hands across her eyes.

How horrible for her to carry this guilt. How did she survive it? "You were just a child. You aren't responsible for the actions of monsters." He skimmed his hands up and down her outer thighs, trying to offer comfort.

"I was eight. Old enough to know not to leave my little sister outside. Old enough to realize I could never catch up to a moving van," she said, voice sounding nearly lifeless now.

"If blame lies anywhere, it's with your parents for leaving two children together unsupervised. Not with a little girl who was just trying to get her sister a drink." How could he possibly get her to see that what had happened was just a tragic event?

"There was a candlelight vigil held in the center of town in her honor. My parents were giving speeches, trying to reason with the people who took her. My grandmother took me to it. As we stood on the grass, she gripped my cheek and stared straight through me." Alex gasped, like a knife had been driven through her side. "She said, 'Look at all the pain you've caused. I wish it had been you instead.' Oh, Jay, I've wished that my whole life. Why couldn't it have been me instead?"

Jay yanked her against his chest, and held her close with all his might, as her body shook with sobs. He swayed her slowly from side to side. A tear trickled down his bare chest, and he angled his head to kiss the top of her head.

"Did your parents know she said that to you?" he muttered into her hair. Her head shook slowly.

"They felt the same, I'm sure of it." When she laid her cheek against his chest, warmth spread through him.

Her admission sparked a slow burn of anger that ran from his Adam's apple to his stomach. How could her family place blame with a child and make her feel responsible? It was unfathomable.

"You're the first person I've ever told. Lindsey knows most, but not all." Her words were merely a whisper. "The guilt is so huge, sometimes when I think of it, I can't draw a breath." She looked up at him with shattered, wide eyes. Her face was red and blotchy from crying.

"Oh, honey." He drew her back in, unable to find the right words despite a career in family counseling. He let her cry it out while holding on to her tight. She fit so perfectly against him, this broken dove, who was locked away in a cold cage of blame and self-reproach.

"She had this giggle." Alex's lips moved against his neck, and goose bumps dashed down his arms. "One that always ended in a snort, like a little piglet. Stephanie had bright blonde hair, so pale it looked nearly white, and the face of a china doll. She always carried around this stupid stuffed elephant she named Ally the Ellie after her best friend. Me." Alex blew out a slow breath, sinking into him as she exhaled. "Ally was abducted with her. I wish I had something, anything to remember her by."

"I know there was an investigation, a search, but did your parents ever hire a private firm?"

"Yes, after a month of waiting for the police investigation. The number of tips and leads started to fall and they reached out to a local firm. They worked for us for about a week, but the cost was so high, my parents couldn't afford it." Alex pulled out of his arms and lowered herself onto the bed. She looked drained and exhausted.

It all made sense to him now. "And that's why you do what you do. Find children, make families whole again." The mattress sagged when he sat on the bed beside her. He knit his fingers together with hers, and she clutched his hand like it was her last tether to sanity.

"The firm makes enough from corporate cases. I won't prey on a family's bank account during their worst time. That's why I hired Gabe, so I could focus more on the missing children cases. Every time there's a positive ending for a family, it gives me a little sliver of redemption, and gives Stephanie's senseless death purpose."

"Why do you feel she's dead?" He smoothed his thumb over her knuckles.

"A beautiful child, like Stephanie? I'd hate to think of what had become of her if she wasn't killed. It's been so long...the chances she survived somehow are not in our favor." Alex kneaded the back of her neck as Hank stirred. The dog meandered over, dropped his head on Alex's lap, and stared at her with a hint of concern. It was about time—Hank could sleep through a heavy metal concert.

With one last kiss on the cheek, he left Alex with Hank and walked to the bathroom. The motels they'd stayed in along the first leg of their journey were purely for convenience, but last night, he wanted them to fall asleep side by side in a more luxurious setting. He put the stopper in the deep Jacuzzi tub and cranked the water on nice and hot. A blanket of foamy bubbles spread over the water as he liberally poured in some of the scented soap left on the quartz countertop.

"I want you to spend an hour relaxing," he said when he returned to the bedroom. Alex looked up at him and tried to brush his hands away when he slid one arm under her thighs and the other around her waist.

"I have two legs," she muttered and squirmed against his hold.

"Let me take care of you." He set her down on the cool marble floor. "Because despite what you believe, you deserve to be cared for. You deserve to be loved." *Let me love you.* Would she, if he told her of the intense ache in his chest when he imagined her slipping out of his life? Or of the swell of happiness that crested and smashed against him at the most random moments—watching her pour an ocean of sugar in her coffee each morning, the way her nose crinkled up when she laughed, her drive to do what was right, and to find what was lost? He leaned around her to turn off the faucet when the bubbles threatened to spill over.

"I can take it from here, unless you were planning on joining me." Alex tried to force a smile, but it fell flat.

"It's more than tempting," he said glancing at the oversized tub just right for two—albeit probably someone smaller than him. "But there's something I need to take care of." He touched his lips to her forehead. "Just take some down time."

Jay shut the bathroom door behind him, changed into

jeans and a T-shirt, and pulled the charging cord from his cell phone. Balmy air scented with pine and earth, softened in last night's rain showers, bathed the room when he opened the balcony slider. He scrolled through his contacts, found Damien's wife Lindsey, and listened to the ringtone.

"Hello?" Lindsey's light, airy voice echoed in his ear, along with the clash of metal against metal, and their Boston terrier Daisy's bark.

"Are you hosting a circus over there?" The corners of his lips tugged into a smile.

"Every day with Maris is a circus, and she's the ring leader." She laughed, then shushed them quiet by saying Mommy was on the phone. "Damien told me you found Luke. What a relief for the whole family. How's he doing?"

"Shaken, but my parents and sisters flew down, so he has support."

"You and Alex are an incredible team to find him so quickly." More clanks and clatters sounded on the other line, but softer this time.

"That's what I'm calling you about: Alex," Jay said.

"Is everything all right?" The concern in her voice was audible as was the quick draw of breath.

"Yes, and no," he said on a sigh. "She told me about her sister. It was heartbreaking, and she mentioned she has nothing to remember her by, nothing to offer her closure or to look back on. I know your paintings mainly steer toward landscapes, but I was thinking if you could do a portrait of them, maybe, I don't know, it would help." The other line was strangely quiet for a moment.

"I wish I thought of it myself. It'll make her cry, but I think it would also be a precious gift. The only problem is I have no idea what Stephanie looked like."

"I googled it before calling. There's a picture of Stephanie from an old news article. Can I email it?" A breeze tickled his skin and puffed up the neck of his shirt.

"That should work. I think there's a picture of Alex as a child on Facebook. I can't make any promises though. I haven't done an oil portrait in a very long time." In the background, Maris was singing about a spider and a waterspout at the top of her lungs.

"Draw up an invoice for me, and I'll get a check over."

Lindsey laughed. "Don't worry, I'll take it easy on you. If I finish it in time, you could give it to her for her birthday on March second. I was thinking of asking everyone over for dinner to celebrate. Oh, and Jay? Welcome to Alex's inner circle. As far as I know, you're the first guy to get there."

When they hung up the phone, Jay made a second call to room service. They'd take another hour to themselves, say their final goodbyes, and hit the road. He'd probably need to do a month of overtime to pay for one of Lindsey's paintings, but it would be worth it to give Alex a piece of her sister back, no matter how small.

Chapter Sixteen

"I'LL FILL UP this seat before my wife has a chance to frighten you off." Jay's father sat in the waiting room chair next to Alex. They'd come back to the hospital to say goodbye to Luke, and Alex had slipped out to give Jay and his nephew a few moments alone.

"There's not much that frightens me anymore, Mr. Hall," she said.

"Ha!" The sergeant slapped his knee, looked at her with approval. "Call me Tom." Alex put a hand on Hank's harness when he sat up and nudged the sergeant's hand, but he reached out and scratched behind the dog's ears. "I don't know how long June rambled on yesterday or what on God's green earth she said. Might've mentioned Rebecca." He paused and raised a questioning brow.

"She did, but only half a dozen times." Alex returned Tom's smile and then busied herself adjusting Hank's harness.

"June likes to romanticize things. Considers it some awful tragedy it didn't work out between two kids. My opinion? She wasn't right for my son. Not much depth to her, not much loyalty."

Her muscles were twitchy, a mix of too much caffeine and old insecurities about the woman Jay swore he was over.

"I'm pleased to see him with a better fit. A partner with some grit." The shoulder squeeze he gave her bordered on painful, but she couldn't deny the swell of gratification in his acceptance. After last night, she was nearly convinced Jay was over his high school love, but she couldn't seem to forget the look in his eyes when he admitted to thinking about her during the moment they'd shared in the tent. Or was she using her own ghosts and the disbelief that she was worthy of love to keep a sliver of distance between her and Jay? She pushed the thought away, scared it was too close to the truth.

"We appreciate what you did to find Luke. What you did to help Amy." Tom held her gaze and patted Hank absently on the head.

"It's good to see him back with his family. Where he belongs." Alex crossed her legs at the ankles and stretched out a bit. They were nearly alone in the waiting room, and Jay was taking longer than she'd expected. Not that she minded. Her conversation with the sergeant was entertaining, and even though it was silly, the little girl she once was basked in the fatherly attention.

"Amy said you won't accept payment for the case. It's admirable. I'd like to give you something of value. A token of our appreciation," he said. On the wall-mounted television, a newscaster was giving the noon update, a freshwater fish tank bubbled in the corner, and Tom smiled down at her with complete admiration.

She swallowed away the increasing tightness in her throat. Maybe it was time to forgive herself. Time to say a final goodbye to her little sister and the memories they'd been robbed of. "There's nothing I need, but if you'd like to make a donation to the Missing Children's Alliance or the Mastiff Rescue League of Boston they'd be grateful for the help."

Tom nodded and was quiet for a moment, fingers circling over Hank's floppy ears. "Next Sunday, once we're back to the Cape, I hope you'll come to dinner. June always makes a nice roast or one of the kids' favorites."

"I've never turned down a home-cooked meal," said Alex, completely charmed by the old vet. "I have to see what the workload is like when I get back to the firm, though."

"How long have you been on your own?" His voice was neutral, but his eyes flickered with concern.

"It seems like a lifetime, but it suits me." Movement near the front desk made her glance up from the invisible patterns she was tracing onto Hank's fur. Jay was near the front desk with his mother and sisters surrounding him. He pulled each one close and hugged them goodbye.

"What about your parents, Alex?" Tom had spotted his family and his lips automatically curved.

"Not really in the picture," Alex said indifferently. Tom's smile disappeared, and his earnest eyes searched her face.

"You've found your place with the Halls." Tom bobbed his head once in a decisive nod.

"Thank you." Alex's throat was far too tight and she fought to choke out the words. A layer of armor was melted off her shoulders as surely as it had been flushed with dragon's breath.

"I was so overwhelmed yesterday, so relieved, I didn't thank you." Amy had walked over to the sitting area and stood in front of Alex with a tissue clutched between both hands. "I guess there's really nothing to summarize how it feels to think you've lost the most important person in your life, and then a complete stranger drops everything to find them." Amy's voice broke and she released a sharp breath. "I can't ever thank you enough for finding my son."

Amy wiped tears away from her cheeks, and Jay came up behind his sister to place two steady hands on her shoulders. This was more than a family, it was a unit. A tightly woven net of support. Could she really ever belong with a family like this, or deserve it? Jay looked down at her, and as if hearing her thoughts, offered a feather-soft smile. The numbness she'd used as emotional anesthesia had begun to wear off, and the prickles of pain mingled with joy and passion moved her. Alex may have found Amy's son, but on this trip with Jay she'd found so much more. She'd found the foothold to forgiveness, trust, and love, and she'd started to climb into the unknown without looking down.

"You really made an impression on the sergeant." Jay shifted his eyes off the road to look over at her from the driver's seat. Behind them, Hank stuck his massive head out the window and sniffed the air, completely in his element on the open road.

"He's a good egg." She leaned back against the headrest and let the warm breeze kiss her skin. It would only take a day or two to get back to New England, so she was going to enjoy the weather and Jay's company as much as she could.

"Until I enlisted, I never really understood what he'd sacrificed. When he missed holidays and birthdays, we'd get sullen and upset. Of course, it sucked—we were just kids. What we didn't realize was it cost him, too. He wanted to be there for us, but he also felt a duty to protect us, and all children." He flicked his gaze to her for a moment. "Without people who are willing to lose those moments for themselves, thousands of families are at stake to lose everything."

Alex shifted slightly in her seat and swallowed a few times. The thinly veiled compliment made her uncomfortable. She wasn't the hero he equated her with in his backward way of offering her praise she wouldn't otherwise accept.

After a moment she cleared her throat. "What stops you from reenlisting?" She looked over the abrasions that raked down his cheek, neck, and upper arm. Her scars were on the inside, while his were in plain sight. He seemed so solid, so confident she never thought of the internal demons he might face because of them.

"I told you about coming home, having my family care for me. It wasn't just the wounds and the physical therapy. I lost some vision in my right eye, too, which would prevent me from going back even if I wanted to. I thought I was getting better, but then the flashbacks started, and I couldn't bring myself to get behind the wheel of a vehicle. I knew about PTSD, knew guys who had it, but for some reason I thought all my mental and physical training would, I don't know, give me some kind of immunity." His jaw tightened, then went lax. "I was wrong."

She understood perfectly and inched her hand over the console to connect her pinkie finger with his, just like he had done at the hospital. A smile hinted on his lips, and he cleared his throat.

"I was prepared to be injured, and I knew there were no guarantees I'd return home with a heartbeat in my chest. Losing someone though—that I wasn't ready for." Jay put on his directional and pulled off the highway. Hank had started to fidget in the back seat, so a break was a good idea.

"Who was he?" Alex traced her little finger over the top of his, enjoying the way his calloused skin rubbed against hers. She knew he understood the question and waited patiently for him to answer.

"Corporal Miller. He was on his last tour before retirement, and in two weeks he was going home to watch his son's high school graduation. Great guy, loved his kids and his wife of twenty-plus years. I had to make a tough decision when the convoy got hit to minimize the loss of life. His was the furthest vehicle, and he was so experienced…" Jay shook his head. "I was wrong, and by the time I got to him, it was too late." They pulled down the exit ramp, and Jay took a left to the more heavily populated side.

Alex wanted to tell him not to blame himself and remind him of the Purple Heart he received from saving three men, but she couldn't bring herself to say the words. Blame was her constant companion. How could she tell Jay he wasn't at fault when she lived and breathed guilt every day? "I'm so sorry. It's hard, and it's unfair."

"It sure is," he said pulling into a parking space in front of a grocery store. "Hang tight." Jay slid out of the driver's seat and took long, purposeful strides to the building. While he was inside, she took the opportunity to clip the leash on Hank and lead him to a grassy area to the side of the building. After sniffing for the perfect spot, he relieved himself and began to lumber back to where they had come from.

By the time Jay got back to the car, Alex and Hank were both sitting back inside with the air conditioner pumping. She raised a brow at the two filled bags he flung into the trunk. "I didn't realize you were going in for groceries." She laughed.

"Just a few things." He put the car in reverse and drove down a side street instead of going back to the main road.

"The highway entrance is back that way," she said, glancing over her shoulder. The green marker disappeared as he continued forward.

"I thought we could stop for lunch first. I don't think my body can handle another drive-through."

She studied him as they drove, curious how he could navigate the area without the use of the GPS. She looked out the window when the tires left the smooth pavement and jumbled along a blanket of pebbles. Outside stretched a wide strip of beach that was nearly secluded. Her insides began to stir when he walked around the car, opened the passenger side door, and held out his hand to her. Something had changed again between them. She could sense it. Now that they were nearing the end of the trip, Jay seemed to take her hand more often and hold her gaze a little longer. All she wanted to do was snuggle against his chest and draw in his fresh scent. Maybe they were both afraid when they reached Massachusetts, everything they had built along the drive would disappear. It was as if they both wanted to ask the other to stay, but neither of them could utter the words.

Alex busied herself getting Hank out of the car while Jay popped the trunk for the grocery bags. Fresh sea air tousled her hair around her face and tugged at her clothing. Together, they walked down the sandy boardwalk and out to the beach. When Jay reached into one of the shopping bags and pulled out a picnic blanket, her stomach tossed like the rolling waves. A gust of wind grabbed the edge of the blue blanket and it settled smoothly over the sand. Jay knelt down and laid out containers of chicken salad, fresh rolls, cheese, crackers, and sliced fruit. A picnic on the beach couldn't be any more out of her comfort zone, but maybe Jay knew that. So many things over the past week had been out of her comfort zone, and she had to admit she was glad.

Alex slipped her shoes off, and the sugary sand seeped between her toes. With a bark of pure joy, Hank ran toward the surf after a band of seagulls. Jay smiled at her, and she was suddenly very aware of the warmth that swirled through her when he was near. Ignoring the quick thump of her heart, she sank down onto the blanket.

"How did you know about this place?" she said as Jay passed her a soda.

"I did some research this morning and took a chance on the directions." He followed her lead, took off his shoes, and sat close enough so one knee was lightly touching hers. "I know you're anxious to get back, but I'm not ready for this to be over yet."

She should be eager to get back to the firm, but suddenly, the mundane routine she'd developed for self-preservation didn't seem like enough. Alex had decisions to make about the kind of future she wanted.

"Who said anything about being in a rush? Gabe can hold the reins for another day or so." Alex took the sandwich Jay handed her and rested it on a napkin. "Maybe this doesn't have to be over when we get back. We could still…hang out." Her cheeks grew hot. Why couldn't she find the right words to tell him she wanted to keep investing time in whatever they had here? He didn't tease her choice of words but nodded in response, as if he could sense her hesitation.

"I'd like that." A smile brightened his face when Hank came barreling down on them, legs soaked from playing in the surf. It might be silly but knowing that Jay loved Hank made her insides go mushy. The oversized pooch was like a child to her, and the first thing she'd put faith in since Stephanie disappeared. What did it mean that she'd now put faith in Jay, too?

He started making a third plate, and the dog's eyes darted back and forth between the containers and the meal being assembled.

Alex halted the bite she was about to take. "Not too much, he'll get car sick."

"Sorry, pal, the warden's watching us." Jay smirked and slid the plate in front of Hank.

"It won't be so amusing when we have to drive all the way back to the Cape with the windows down to escape the smell of dog throw up."

"I'll cut him a break. I've gotten a bit attached to him on the drive. To his mom, too." He reached his hand up to her face to smooth back a strand of hair that had been tucked behind her ear. His words made her feel drunk, disoriented and warm, alive and invincible.

"What are we doing here, Jay?" she mumbled as he leaned closer to her. Tingles raced down her spine when he trailed his fingers down her cheek and neck.

"Falling in love, I think." His breath played over her lips, and he touched them lightly with his. A jolt shot through her. Oh my God. Love? Alex suspected she'd already fallen, but to hear him speak the words that invaded her mind at least ten times a day made her body go weak. Jay kissed her forehead, then her eyelids, before trailing slowly back to her mouth. She inhaled, filling her lungs with the smell of salt, seaweed, and Jay's fresh aftershave. It could have been seconds, minutes, or days that they kissed. She no longer could concentrate on mundane tasks like keeping track of time. Then he pulled away, but only to stare into her eyes for a few moments. A blur of color shimmered within her line of sight, and she turned toward the water. The sparse breath she had left in her lungs whooshed out of her.

"Oh, wow." The sound of her voice could've easily been stolen by the wind if Jay wasn't sitting so close. His knee rubbed against hers as he tensed, then relaxed. They sat hand in hand, just marveling at the three majestic animals that strolled along the beach, a parade of copper and gold with creamy sea-swept manes. Even Hank sat like a statue as the wild horses meandered along in the surf.

"They're incredible," Jay said in a low, awestruck voice. The largest whinnied, shook out its mane, and snorted, tossing its head to the sky. A silver foal stayed close to the smaller of the two adults, taking cautious steps near the water. After a few moments, he got bolder and waded further into the water. When the next wave hit, the little horse stumbled. Alex gasped as the sizable wave tried to drag him into the ocean. His mother nudged him away from the surf, and they continued to walk along the beach.

"That's how you make me feel, Alex. Like I've been swept out to sea by the current. I never can quite catch my footing or tread long enough before you pull me deeper." Jay's voice, gruff and heavy, touched a hidden cord inside her chest, and her soul sang.

Little did he know she was the one left with lungs burning for air, because she could scarcely breathe as her heart stammered, and was lost.

Chapter Seventeen

Another seven hundred miles on the road and they hit Massachusetts. They did their ritual high-five as they crossed state lines, and Alex sighed beside him.

"Relieved to be home?" Jay didn't want his time with her to end, even though everything he was feeling was impractical, dangerous. When he mentioned he thought they were falling in love on the beach, he had lied. He was already there. How had it happened so quickly? It could have been the intensity of the situation or his gratitude toward her that was fueling his feelings, but that wouldn't explain why his stomach turned to stone each time he pictured Alex slipping out of his life. Why his adrenaline spiked and his heart began to explode out of his chest when he thought of her SUV driving away from the Cape and back to her Boston firm.

"Not there yet—don't jinx us," she said, and changed the station on the radio.

Part of him yearned to ask her what happened next for them, to demand she stay in his life. The other more practical part urged him to take it slow. If he held too tight, he'd shatter what they'd built and if he pressed her to share her feelings, she might panic and run. Hank popped up from the back seat to see what was going on; then content that Alex was still in the car, he nestled back against the cushions. They drove in relative silence the rest of the way to Jay's cottage, and by the time they arrived it was nearly morning. The post lamp was on, illuminating the crushed seashell driveway.

Alex put the car in park and shut off the ignition. The silence grew heavy in the space between them, as they both searched for something to say.

"I'll help you with your stuff." Alex opened her door and jumped to the ground. He only had a duffel bag, which he could easily take himself. He got out and opened the door to the back seat for Hank.

"He could use a bathroom break and a bowl of water." Jay found himself giving the dog a quick kiss on his massive forehead, and Hank lapped his face. He'd grown attached to the slobbery beast, too. Alex came around the car holding his bag.

"I'll take it." He reached out to slip the duffel out of her hands. Their skin touched and an electric current raced down his back. Alex must've felt it too, because she drew her hands away and thrust them into her back pockets. Unspoken words and racing thoughts had put a barrier between them. Who was going to be the first to shatter the wall by asking about the future? He fumbled for the key, unlocked the dead bolt, and walked into the dark hallway. Jay held the door open for Alex and whistled for Hank who was sniffing along the tree line. The dog loped up to the door and lumbered in to take a look at the new surroundings.

"I'll get the water for Hank. Want anything?" He switched on a few lights so she could find her way around without tripping over something.

"I could use a water, too. Thanks." She rocked back on her heels and watched Hank explore the living room.

The house was spacious for one, but it suited him. There was a little pond out back with two weeping willows, and the stillness of the water and the sigh of wind ruffling the tree branches soothed him. He hadn't needed three bedrooms, the gleaming hardwood floors, or the airy living room with a stone fireplace, but he had needed the serenity that the view off the deck brought to him.

Under the kitchen counter he found a large red bowl he usually used for popcorn and filled it up with water before unearthing a glass for Alex. He walked slowly to avoid water sloshing over the sides of the bowl, placed it on the tiled hall floor, and went to look for Alex. He found her on the light gray sectional and warmth spread through his chest. Sitting up against the arm of the couch with her baggy sweatshirt stretched over her knees, she looked like she belonged in his space. Alex was the first woman to be in his house besides his mother and sisters, and she just fit, like the two end tables that complemented the couch.

"You have a great place," Alex said and reached up for

her water. "It's really cozy." Her eyes traced over the family photos and simple decorations that Amy had insisted were masculine and completely necessary for the top of the mantel. He'd grown to like the wrought-iron lanterns.

Jay laughed. "My sisters made sure I didn't move into a cave. They framed the pictures for the walls and did some shopping."

"Something told me you wouldn't have sought out throw pillows." She grinned over her glass. Hank made himself comfortable by jumping up on the couch and lay down right in the middle of them.

"Your bodyguard is here," Jay teased, and scratched behind his floppy ear.

"Sometimes I swear he can hear what I'm thinking." She took a sip of water, placed it on the coffee table, and circled her arms around her knees. "It's like he knows I didn't want to come inside, because the other part of me wanted you to ask me to stay so badly." She whispered the words, and his pulse lunged against his skin. Did Alex know he understood what it cost her to be vulnerable? It cost him too, but he was willing to go there. With her.

"What do you want to do, Lex? Where do you want this to go?" He reached over Hank to take her hand.

"I don't know what you've done to me," she said quietly. "My head is a chaotic, disorganized mess when we're together. I've forgotten to check in with Gabe more than once during our drive, and half the time I can't catch my breath."

Her words touched the deepest part of him, and his soul trembled.

"I know the feeling." He gave her hand a gentle squeeze.

"No, I don't think you do. I don't sleep with clients. Ever. I don't date, or plan for the future, or feel these...these feelings." She spat out the words as if they tasted bad, and he nearly laughed at the way her lips were set in a pouty frown. "I didn't want to feel this way, but with you, the control has been stripped from me." She shook her head and looked at her knees. "I couldn't get a handle on this if I tried."

"So, you're saying you care, but you're not happy about it." His cheek twitched as his lips fought to curve.

"That's exactly what I'm saying. I haven't done a real relationship, Jay, and I don't know what to do or say. I'm bound to screw up and throw it all to hell. I don't want to hurt you, or let you hurt me." Alex sighed and rubbed her temples.

"You shouldn't have such little faith in yourself. I spent half of the return ride racking my brain for the right words, and you just summed everything up perfectly. I wasn't looking for this either, Lex, but now I don't want to let it go." He held her gaze and those rich, whiskey eyes were wide and exposed. A quiet message passed between them, one that needed no words to understand. She was gifting him with her trust, just as he was to her. In one graceful motion Alex untucked her legs and skirted around the snoring dog.

She climbed into his open arms and he pulled her close

against him. The beat of her heart thrummed against his skin, and he captured her lips in a deliberately unhurried kiss. They didn't need to rush; they had time to take things slow. As long as Alex was with him, Jay didn't need every promise or commitment mapped out. They'd find their own way, even if they stumbled blindly.

"You know I need to go back to Boston, right?" Alex murmured and rested her head against his chest. "I don't care about the apartment. I never really made it a home—it's just a place to sleep, but the firm is something I've built from the ground up."

"Being together doesn't mean we have to change who we are and what we've built. We've both worked hard enough to do that as is. How about for now, we just agree to make time for each other? I can drive up to Boston for a night or two, and when you have a free weekend here and there, you and Hank can stay with me at the Cape." He touched the silky strands of her hair, starting at the crown and moving over the tips. Alex brought her hands up and tucked both under her cheek. Her sweetness was unraveling him as she snuggled into his side.

"I'm going to leave soon and see what's happening at the firm. I'm sure I have a zillion emails and new cases to sort through, but maybe on Sunday I'll come down and we can go to your parents' house for dinner, and I'll spend the night."

"That sounds perfect, and Hank is always welcome at

their place too. My mom will spoil him rotten." He continued stroking her hair, enjoying the weight of her against him. A few minutes passed, and her breathing deepened. When he glanced down, her eyes were closed and her lips were slightly parted. Jay smiled and kissed the top of her head. He shifted slowly so he didn't wake her and scooped her up.

"Come on, Hank. Bedtime." The dog's nails clicked against the floor as he followed Jay to the bedroom. He laid Alex down, unlaced her shoes, and tucked her under the thick down comforter. Jay patted the bed to give Hank the okay to jump up. Despite Hank's large frame, the bed was big enough for the three of them. Jay threw on sweatpants and a T-shirt and slid under the covers beside Alex. Even in sleep she curled in to him and circled her arm over his torso. He took a large breath savoring her clean, citrus scent. Against the plush mattress with Alex in his arms, his worries dissipated, leaving his mind and body weightless. He would follow Alex anywhere, but for now he closed his eyes, hugged her close, and followed her into sleep.

Chapter Eighteen

"I'm starving," Alex said as they pulled up to the traditional blue-shuttered colonial. Was it hunger or nerves that rendered her stomach a choppy mess? She'd met his parents already—the hard part was over—so why did it seem so important to make a good impression now? Hank panted with excitement as he stared out the window.

"My mom will change before you take off your coat." Jay chuckled. She'd missed his laugh. Heck, she'd missed everything about him during the workweek. Even Hank seemed to lose the spring in his step. They weren't really in a long-distance relationship, but it sure felt like it after being in the close quarters of the car. Alex grasped the bottle of wine and opened her door. They walked hand in hand up the circular drive with Hank trotting at their side. Before they could even reach the front step, the door swung open, and June was standing in the threshold with oven mitts on both hands and a coordinating Williams Sonoma apron tied around her waist.

"I've been so looking forward to seeing you again." June crushed her into a powerful hug and flour puffed into the air from her clothes. "The rest of the kids are all here, Amy and Luke and Courtney and Ashley. They're all sitting in the living room having some snacks, so make yourself at home."

Hank must have heard the word *snacks*, because he squeezed by Jay's mom and into the house. Alex cleared her throat. "Thank you for having me." She offered June the bottle of wine.

"Oh, so lovely. Thank you, dear. And it's nice to see you too, honey," she said, finally acknowledging her son before she retreated into the house so they could come inside.

"Uh-huh, I see where I stand," Jay teased and looped his right arm around his mom's shoulders and gave her a quick squeeze. Heat trickled through her chest. This was the type of family bond she'd dreamed of having after Stephanie was taken and everything crumbled. There was a sudden thickness in her throat, as a melancholy feel settled over her. "Anything we can help with?" Jay asked.

"Oh, no. Go sit with the others. After all, I only get to cook on Sundays." June looked from Jay to her. "My kids can only make time for their aging parents once a week," she said on a theatrical sigh.

Jay cast his eyes to the ceiling and someone let out a long, dramatic groan from the next room.

"Leave 'em alone or they'll only come once a month," Tom grumbled. He put down the chair he was carrying and leaned in to give Alex a kiss on the cheek. "Good to see you, sweetheart."

Alex had never been welcomed so warmly, and she swallowed the hard lump in her throat. Jay gripped her hand and led her into the living room. A fire roared in the brick hearth and Hank stretched out right in front of it to reap its warmth. Even though a large sage-colored couch and two accent chairs were arranged around the fireplace, the others were lounging on the floor around a game of Monopoly centered on a light oak coffee table.

"Good to see you again." Alex recognized the gorgeous woman who spoke as Jay's older sister, Courtney. A long sweep of blonde hair trailed over her shoulders and another woman sat on her lap. "This is my girlfriend, Ashley," she said and ruffled the top of her brown cropped hair.

"Ash has been part of the family nearly as long as Luke," Jay said giving all the girls a peck on the top of the head.

"How's my favorite nephew?" Jay moved some of the pillows and board games off the couch so they could sit.

"I'm your only nephew," Luke said rolling his eyes but smiling all the same. He looked great for someone who had been kidnapped and dragged through the forest of the Blue Ridge Mountains. Jay had told her Luke and Amy had moved in with their parents for the time being, for the additional stability and support. Ashley let out a whoop when Courtney landed on the Go to Jail square at the corner of the board.

"This is going to be my lucky day." Ashley shook two dice in her hands and tossed them onto the table. "Hah!" she yelled with a smile and moved the silver Scottie dog around the game. She purchased the boardwalk for four hundred dollars, lining the left side of the board with little red hotels.

"What are the stakes, today?" Jay sat on the couch with Alex, and the well-worn piece of furniture sagged under his weight. They must have had many fun game nights in this living room, popcorn and movies, Christmases spent gathered around a sparkling balsam fir.

"Losers are on dish duty." Amy took her turn and moved the top hat piece two spaces. "And it's starting to look like that will be me, Luke, and Court."

Jay helped himself to a pita wedge and dip that sat near the Monopoly board and lifted the glass serving dish to offer her some. The savory spinach and artichoke dip was still warm and layered with cheese. It was so delicious she immediately swiped another piece of bread through it.

"Don't let me get the recipe for this," Alex said to Jay before taking another bite of the pita. Everyone laughed and Alex smiled as wide as she could with a full mouth.

"It's no joke. Either you have crazy fast metabolisms or you've learned how to step away from your mom's cooking." Ashley looked from Courtney, to Amy, and then to Jay. "But for outsiders like us, something called the Sunday seventeen happens. Consider yourself warned and pick up a few pairs of stretch pants." Ashley grinned at Alex, and the tension that had built up between her shoulder blades eased. She wasn't sure what she had expected, but it wasn't this easy camaraderie and relaxed atmosphere. Maybe because she also considered herself somewhat of a misfit, she'd taken Shane's words to heart when Jay told him his family could give him money in exchange for Luke. *How nice of you to remind me. You never let me forget it when I was a kid. Just some loser who knocked up his girlfriend.*

No, this wasn't the stuffy, judgmental family she imagined. She'd had a taste of their kindness in the hospital but didn't really believe she could belong—until now as they sat around the table with June fussing over each of them. Even Hank had been given a plate, which was now licked clean.

"Alex, take more potatoes. Jay tells me you're a runner like him." Jay's mother came around the table with the casserole dish and loaded her up with a second helping of mashed potatoes filled with cheese, chives, and overall goodness. "There," June said finally looking satisfied that she wouldn't starve. "With a business to look after you need to keep up your strength." Then she moved on to pushing seconds on the rest of the table.

Luke chuckled and winked at Alex. He'd forewarned her that June would relentlessly keep her plate piled high like an all-you-can-eat buffet. At the end of the table, Courtney cleared her throat and grasped Ashley's hand. "We have a little bit of news," she said, eyes never leaving Ashley's face. June sucked in a breath and the chatter and clatter of dishes and silverware stilled. All eyes turned to them, and they both blushed.

"Yesterday, I asked Ashley to marry me. She said yes!" Courtney reached into her pocket and pulled out a princess-cut diamond. June made a sound Alex could only describe as pure delight, and Luke held up his hands as if to shield his eyes. "Jeez, that thing's huge. It's blinding me."

She should feel like an intruder on this intimate family moment, but instead she admired the ring and congratulated the newly engaged couple along with everyone else. A blur caught the corner of her eye, and she looked over her shoulder to see Tom disappearing around the corner. Her scalp prickled and she sat up a little straighter. Was Courtney's father upset about the union? Alex leaned to the right, trying to see where he'd escaped to.

"And the best part is Amy and Jay helped to pick out the ring a few days ago. It was like fate that they had her exact size, so I popped the question a week early." Courtney's bubbly voice brought her back to reality.

"What's wrong?" Jay's breath tingled against her skin. She had an overactive imagination; Tom probably left to use the bathroom.

"Where did your dad go?" she whispered back to him, and Jay shrugged in response.

"Congratulations!" Tom shouted, startling her and everyone else in the room. There was a loud pop and she flinched as something wet misted over her skin. Champagne fizzed from the bottle he held, face lit like a jovial jack-o'-lantern on Halloween. A huge breath rushed out of her lungs and a shaky laugh seeped from her lips. Maybe she carried more trauma from her volatile childhood than she realized. Her parents had never physically hurt her, but they had terrifying fights after Stephanie was taken, and she'd slept in her closet more than one night to avoid noise.

Being with Jay's family made her pity the girl she once was. All this time she'd blamed herself—and a piece of her still did—but she deserved more love and care than her parents were able to provide. Could she finally accept that she deserved to be with someone as kind and heroic as Jay? She looked up to steal a glance at his face, and he was already looking down at her with a silly grin on his face, and in front of everyone he lifted her chin and planted a kiss on her mouth. There were hoots of laughter and a gagging sound from Luke. Her face burned from the apples of her cheeks to the tips of her ears, and when she locked eyes with Jay, faith in the possibility of what they were building threaded between them.

After flutes of champagne were circulated, stories of the proposal were exchanged, and white chocolate raspberry cheesecake was reduced to a single sliver of crust, Alex and Jay said their goodbyes with promises to come back next Sunday.

"That wasn't too bad was it?" Jay gave her one of the light shoulder bumps she'd come to expect when he was in a playful mood. Hank trotted ahead of them and waited patiently to be let into the back seat of the car.

"The opposite. When I told your mom I wanted to come back next Sunday, it wasn't to be polite. It's something I'll look forward to." She put her hands against his chest when they stopped in front of the passenger door.

"God, that's good to hear." He angled his head to meet her lips, and a shock zinged through her at the slightest caress of skin against skin.

After a few moments, she broke the kiss and sighed. "As much as I'm enjoying this, we should take it back to your place."

"Worried about my mom and her infrared binoculars?"

"You say it as a joke, but I wouldn't be surprised." She opened the truck door, Hank plodded in, and Alex followed the dog up into the cab.

"No, I've come to expect that sort of thing from her." Jay joined her in the truck and gave her one more kiss that turned her muscles to melted butter. She sighed and leaned back against the seat. This had been the best evening she'd had in a very long time, and now she was going to spend the night wrapped in Jay's arms. It really couldn't get any better.

Chapter Nineteen

JAY FOLDED OVER an omelet and sprinkled shredded cheese on top. He slid it onto a plate, added a few strips of bacon, and buttered toast. He turned to Alex, and his heart skipped a beat. She sat at the table, holding a mug of coffee with both hands, and watched him with a content smile. Morning sunlight streamed through the kitchen window and illuminated her fresh, makeup-free face. Gold freckles dusted the bridge of her nose and matched the gilded highlights illuminating her glossy hair. He was completely done for.

"Order up." He couldn't resist leaning down to brush her lips as he set the plate down.

She took a bite and sighed. "Now that I know you can cook, you might never get rid of me."

"In that case, I'll give my two weeks at Veterans' Services and be your personal line cook." He couldn't wipe the stupid grin off his face. What had Alex done to him? A cold, wet tongue lapped his wrist and he looked down into Hank's pleading eyes and offered him some bacon.

"He's not going to want to go home." Alex smiled over her steaming mug of coffee and took a careful sip.

"He's always welcome as long as he brings his mom." He held her gaze for one breath, then two as hope and trust saturated the air. He wanted to share his home with her. To see her clothes strewn amongst his in the laundry basket and her toothbrush on the side of the sink. He could envision them sitting on the deck to talk about their days, and watch Hank play in the pond. Maybe they'd even get another dog. The shrill chirp of Alex's phone startled them both, and Alex dropped her fork.

"Sorry, this might be Gabe. He's supposed to send me some files later." Alex pushed back the chair and went to get her phone off the kitchen island. When she looked down at the screen, a frown settled on her face. "Huh," she grunted. "It's my mom."

As Alex's face paled, Jay's stomach tensed.

"Hello?" Alex said with uncharacteristic unease riding her voice like a wave. She started to pace the tile floor on bare feet, one hand holding the iPhone and the other crossed over her chest. Jay tried to give her some privacy and turned back to his breakfast, but the hysterical crying on the other line echoed through the quiet kitchen.

"How could you say I don't care? You're not the only one who lost her." Alex's voice hissed through her teeth. She stopped in front of the glass slider that led to the backyard and stared out with an expression that held something more than pain, more than profound suffering.

"Every year since I moved out I've called—" Her head

was bent down and she pressed her hand to her forehead, as Jay considered what to do that would best help Alex. Interrupt the call? Go stand beside her?

"Don't you know I wish that every day?" Alex shouted into the phone, voice on the brink of breaking. "If it had been me, I wouldn't wake up thinking everything is fine until reality punches me in the face. You have no idea. No clue what it's like to carry the responsibility." Alex threw her hand to the side in a gesture of utter exhaustion.

Okay. That was enough. He could only handle seeing so much of Alex's pain. He jumped up and the chair legs thudded against the floor. He put his hand on her shoulder, and the material of her baby-soft sweater pressed against his skin. "Take a deep breath, Lex," he whispered, and before she could protest, he slid the phone from her hand, jerked open the slider and stepped out into the cleansing morning air.

"Mrs. Macintyre," he said in a deep growl, planting his feet on the ground in a wide stance.

"Who's this? Where's my daughter?" said a shrill, nearly manic voice on the other end of the line. A cabinet slammed and a television buzzed in the distance.

"I'm someone who cares for her. Really cares. She's taking a break from whatever toxic information you're feeding her. The conversation I heard may have been one-sided, but it was enough to tell me you were giving her one hell of a guilt trip."

"Put her back on. This has nothing to do with you." Something crashed, then shattered.

"That's not going to happen," he said with a breath in through his nose and out through his mouth, as he harnessed his calm. "I'm sorry for what your family went through, but you had two daughters, and you made the decision to place blame on an eight-year-old. What made Stephanie more special, that you wish Alex had been taken instead?" A vein in his neck pulsed as he fought for control.

There was a sharp inhale of breath. "I…Stephanie, she was my baby. If Alex hadn't left her—"

The surge of anger rushed through him, heating his blood like an industrial furnace housed in a closet. "How about if you hadn't left a child caring for another child? Or is that thought too painful, too much to bear, so it was easier to lay blame and strip away what was left of Alex's childhood?" A gut-wrenching sob pulsated against his eardrum and he held the phone away, but he couldn't stop the stream of words. She needed to see how wrong she was. "It would have broken anyone else, but Alex has strong shoulders—she's handled the weight of it—and a tough mind. She's as solid as a soldier. Despite the odds you stacked against her, she made something of herself. Dedicates her life to finding missing people. How could you not be proud of that?"

There was no answer, only weeping. "I'm going to hang up and go take care of your daughter. The one who's left."

He jabbed the red circle to hang up and released a long

breath. Despite the chill in the air, the ice on his pond was beginning to melt. In the summer, he and Alex could build a fire in the stone pit or take out a kayak. They could put on their swimsuits and take a cooler to the dog-friendly beach down the street. He just wanted to be with her, and right now he wanted to heal her hurts. He stepped up onto the deck and went back in the house where Hank greeted him, with a frenzied whine. He could hear the reason why. Alex was crying upstairs.

"Okay, boy. I'll take care of it." He patted Hank on the head and started toward the stairs. The click of nails on wood followed behind him.

In his bedroom, he found Alex gathering her things and jamming them into her backpack. She looked up at him with swollen, red-rimmed eyes, then down at the T-shirt she'd folded. Actions were always better than words with Alex. The carpet cushioned his feet as he walked around the bed to her and brought his arms around her. She tried to wiggle away, but he held her until she buried her head against his chest and cried with a quiet whimper. She pulled back and looked at him with haunted eyes. "Yesterday was the anniversary of Stephanie's disappearance. I make myself call each year, to make sure they're okay, but I forgot. Everything just felt so normal spending time with your family. How could I forget something like that?"

"Don't beat yourself up, Lex. The roles should be reversed. They should be picking up the phone each year to make sure you're okay. That's what good parents do." He ran his hands up and down her back, loving how her body fit firmly against his.

Alex shook her head. "Before you, I would've been able to shield myself from my mother's not-so-subtle barbs, but I'm not the same person I was two weeks ago. You've opened something in me, softened my defenses. Ones I thought I was ready to live without." Alex stepped back and an ache settled in the back of his throat. He tried to swallow, but it only intensified the discomfort.

"You made me vulnerable, Jay." She opened her mouth, then closed it. "When we were on the road, just the two of us, I thought I was ready for this, that a relationship might work between us. I was wrong and it's a shame because you're the best man I know. I just can't keep opening myself up." More tears spilled from the corners of her eyes and trailed over skin that was washed of all color.

"Don't make this about us." Sour bile burned over the top of his tongue as she disconnected from him on both an emotional and physical level. His fingers chilled and a tingling sensation swarmed in his chest. "This is about you and your parents and about forgiving yourself for something that wasn't your fault. This is about me being someone you can count on to have your back and pushing me away because you don't think you deserve it."

"That's right. I'm the one who's fucked up, Jay." Her shoulders slumped and for the first time, Alex looked utterly defeated.

"No," he said sternly and grasped her hand. "I'm not giving up on you, Lex. You need to let it go. Your sister, your shitty parents, your misplaced guilt. Get over it. Rise above it." A pained look swept over her face and his belly knotted. Those weren't the words he'd meant to say. Get over it? What horrible advice. He struggled to fill his lungs and searched his mind for a way to apologize or rephrase what he meant.

"Get over it?" Her voice wavered and rose an octave.

"You need to let the past go. I know it's hard, because I've had to do it, too. Of course, I think of Corporal Miller, his kids, his wife but then I put it in the back of my mind because destroying my life over what could've been isn't going to bring him back. I've let go of the anger toward my best friend and Becky, and you know what? I found someone who truly gets me. Who I love more than I thought possible. I'm not the same person I was two weeks ago either." Alex stilled, and her hand went rigid in his. For the second time he regretted his words, not because he didn't love her, but because now sheer panic glazed her wide eyes.

"Maybe you think you're in love with me," she murmured, voice breathless. "But how could you be when you don't understand the most basic part of me? I know you've suffered too, but don't mistake your situation, your feelings with mine. I've held on to this since I was eight years old. I didn't have the love and support of a family to help me work through it. If I let go of what happened, it will be like letting go of Stephanie. Like I'm admitting she's gone forever. That such a bright light was snuffed out so senselessly." Alex laid one hand on Hank's head and swung one strap of her bag over her shoulder.

"Why? Would it be confirming something you already know? Or do you think you deserve to feel guilty forever?" His voice shook as he desperately tried to rein in the argument.

"I need to go," she said flatly and looked at him with her chin raised in defiance.

"We're going to finish this." His patience was frayed, just as his heart was unraveling in his chest. He blocked her way out and a low snarl ripped from Hank's throat. Jay stepped back as an abrupt coldness hit at his core. The dog, ever loyal to Alex, was blocking him out too and their trio was divided. He stepped to the side and let them pass but before they walked out of the room, he tried one last time.

"I deal with PTSD, and I'm not embarrassed to say I've seen someone for it. Taken medication for it. Sometimes there are no answers, and you have to find a way to make peace. Leave if you want, but take care of yourself. You deserve to be taken care of. See someone, Lex—it'll help." He said the last words quietly. Every muscle in his body was drained and the sluggish beat of his heart made him dizzy and disoriented.

Alex gave him one long last look and marched down the stairs and out the front door.

Chapter Twenty

THE FUZZY WHINE didn't register to Alex. She sat on the couch with her legs crossed under her, staring at the black television screen. She hadn't been to work in three days, nor did she answer Gabe's relentless calls to make sure she was all right or to update her on new cases. She supposed he deserved a raise for running her business.

She was still drained from the hysterical sob fest on Monday night. When she'd finally parked her car in the apartment's garage, she'd banged her fists against the steering wheel before bawling into Hank's fur. The guttural sound echoing through the car startled her, until she realized it ripped from her own throat. How stupid she'd been to think she and Jay could have something lasting after just two weeks. The brevity of their time together did nothing to ease the sickening spasm in her stomach.

When she was with Jay, she forgot some of the grief, and for once, things weren't so heavy. Only now, in her simple shell of a home, where the only picture she hung was of Hank, could she admit she loved Jay. She didn't see that changing, but maybe someday she'd get to a point where the memories were sweet instead of searing agony.

There was a knock at the door, and she groaned. Why didn't Gabe understand she didn't want Chinese, or pizza, or any other takeout he'd tried to thrust on her? She pushed herself off the couch and took her time walking to the door. On a deep breath, Alex slid open the latch. New tears she thought herself incapable of burned against the backs of her eyelids when she saw Lindsey standing in the doorway with a plate full of homemade cupcakes.

"Oh, Alex. I'm so sorry your mom called, and that you fought with Jay." Her eyes were warm and sincere. Lindsey was one of the nicest people she'd ever met.

She tossed her purse on the armchair and joined Alex on the couch. Lindsey quietly passed her a vanilla cupcake frosted with green sprinkles and purple sugar.

"Maris wanted to decorate them, and she made me promise you'd eat that one first. Then the red one, then the blue." Lindsey chuckled softly.

"Is she trying to put me out of my misery with sugar shock?" She didn't have an appetite, but she took a bite because it would be rude not to. Once she did, her stomach growled and she realized how little she'd eaten in the past few days.

Lindsey peeled down the wrapper on hers and sampled it. "Do you want to tell me about the argument? Maybe it will help to step back and look at it from a different angle," she said over a mound of frosting. As an artist, that's what

Lindsey did best. She found the right perspective and breathed life into every canvas she touched.

"My mother called and laid on a heaping dose of guilt. Jay took the phone from me, and I'm not sure what was said, but that wasn't the part that angered me." Someone had finally stuck up for her and it scared her more than she cared to admit. If she let another person fight her battles, would she forget how? She paused to polish off her cupcake, crumpled up the wrapper, and sent it soaring toward the little wastebasket in the hall. It missed its mark, but she didn't care enough to stand up and retrieve it.

"What then?" Lindsey asked and got up to put the wrapper in the trash.

"I mentioned my sister, and he said I needed to let it go and move on with my life. I've lived with this remorse so long; it's part of me. And what would happen if I stopped feeling sorry? If I moved on? It would be like saying goodbye to Steph all over again, admitting that she's gone for good." Alex let out a deep sigh and unfolded the thick blanket draped over the side of the couch. She pulled it close, trying to drive back the cold.

"I can understand why you'd feel that way. It's a really tough situation." Lindsey leaned in closer and rested her elbows on her knees.

"That's not all. He told me he loved me. Maybe the cramped quarters in the car and the high-stress situation made him feel more than he actually does, because if he had real feelings for me, wouldn't he be able to understand why I feel so responsible for my sister—and not only that but my entire family unraveling?" Her stomach rolled and not because she'd downed two cupcakes in under five minutes.

"That's a lot of burden to carry." Lindsey adjusted the blanket over Alex's bare feet. "If the roles were reversed, and Jay lost his sister, wouldn't you want him to live on, despite what had happened?"

"Of course," Alex sighed. "But it's different. The only thing that keeps me sane is helping other people, so they don't experience the horrors we did. It's ingrained in who I am."

"I know. I think Jay's heart was in the right place, that he was only thinking of your feelings and your self-preservation. He came over this morning," she said and bit her lower lip. "He looked miserable. He never said he wanted you to stop helping people, Alex, or stop being yourself…only to stop beating yourself up over the past and realize that you deserve happiness. Don't you think that's true?"

"Is that supposed to make me feel better? That I hurt him?" She snapped out the words and hated herself for the ugly tone but Lindsey didn't flinch.

"No. It was meant to show you that he cares for you, deeply, and you're not the only one who's wounded. Maybe you should text him, Alex. I've never seen you undone by a man before. Maybe this is something you can talk through."

A hard lump clogged Alex's throat. "Lindsey," she said

with a hint of desperation in her voice. "I purposely shoved him away." She shook her head, looked down at her hands, and shifted to draw her knees closer to her chest.

"Why?" Lindsey gently prodded.

"Because I love him too, and I'm scared to be vulnerable. I guess I've never felt like I really deserve to be happy for all the pain I've triggered, and I definitely didn't do anything to deserve a man half as wonderful as Jay." Alex let out a groan and rested her head in her hands. She needed time and solitude to make sense of her jumbled feelings and decide how she wanted to move forward with the rest of her life.

"Give yourself a break." Lindsey touched her shoulder with a reassuring smile. "People come to you from all over to help them find missing children and lost pets."

"Ugh, why do you have to be so nice all the time?" she said with no real anger behind it. Lindsey only chuckled.

Lindsey's hands moved in comforting, circular motions around her back, but it did nothing to ease the ache in her heart for her sister, and for Jay. She was beginning to realize how foolish she'd been. He wanted her to put aside her past to protect her, not to judge her for harboring the guilt and shame of her sister's disappearance.

Had she used the disagreement as an opportunity to justify pushing him away to avoid any more pain? Her stomach plummeted. She'd jumped at the first chance to walk out of his life to avoid being hurt. Hadn't he showed her hundreds of times that he was a helper and a nurturer despite his dangerous appearance? She exhaled and massaged her throbbing temples. She'd used his one slip—the let-it-go comment—against him, to justify her running away from the best thing that had ever happened to her. All because she was scared.

"Come on, let's order some pizza. I know you have a bottle of wine or some beers lying around here." Lindsey took her hand and squeezed. "When's the last time we had a sleepover?"

"You're not going to put cucumbers over my eyes and make me do green face treatments, right?"

"Probably not." Lindsey laughed. "Where are your take-out menus?" She started to get off the couch, and Alex flicked her eyes to the ceiling in pretend exasperation.

"What decade is this? Just pick a place from your phone. Maria's has the best mozzarella sticks." She looked down and Hank was licking his chops.

"Now you're talking my language." Lindsey called in the order and stood up to get something from her purse.

"Here." She held out a brochure for an art gallery exhibit and silent auction. "I was really hoping you'd come to my first show. It might be nice to get out of the house, but if you're not feeling up to it, I'd understand."

Alex turned the brochure over. "I'm so proud of you. I wouldn't miss it for the world."

"Thank you," Lindsey squealed and wrapped her in a big hug. "I promise it will be an event you'll never forget, but back to the important topic. Please tell me you'll think about talking to Jay. You guys could work it out, you know."

Alex choked down fresh tears that threatened to fall. "I think I need to work on myself first."

Chapter Twenty-One

LAUGHTER AND GIGGLES erupted from the shoreline as Damien's sister, Kate, and Maris, bundled in thick coats and woolen hats, ran from the dark whitecaps that foamed over the beach. Even the rhythm of the rocking waves and the bracing gusts of wind that carried the scent of salt and brine didn't soothe the scald in his chest. It had been days since he'd spoken to or seen Alex. He returned to work and while he was physically there, his mind was in other places. His focus on tasks wavered as he imagined the sound of her husky laugh, her dry sense of humor, and the lemony scent of her skin. It was pure torment.

"Dude, you're a fucking disaster." Damien's windbreaker ruffled in a squall that rode over the ocean and onto the beach. They sat on a sandy slope close enough for his friend to keep an eye on his daughter, even though Kate was more than capable. "Go talk to her. Tell her you're sorry—whatever it takes, right?"

"Alex can't move past her sister being abducted—not just that, she blames herself." He rolled his shoulders back to ease the ache that rested between them. "It's hard to watch the torment she carries and not be able to help her. She won't let me help." Jay dug his fingers into the powder-soft sand. "Until she's ready for that, there's nothing I can do. You know that. We see it all the time with the guys who come through our door."

"You can't fix everyone, but you can give her something no one else has. You could stand by her. Put faith in her. Where others have blamed and isolated her, you could lift her up and show her that a real family stays and works things out. Just like Lindsey did for me." Damien jumped to his feet as Maris ran too close to the water, but Kate swooped in and curled her up, showering her face with kisses. His friend, who had changed and grown so much since their first meeting, lowered back onto the sand.

"I told her I loved her, and she walked away." He tried to ignore the tightness in his chest and the chill in his limbs. It was like Alex had taken the warmth with her when she left.

"Someone kind of smart told Lindsey that rarely are things so broken they can't be fixed." Those were Jay's own words spoken on the day Lindsey had appeared at his office with tears in her eyes to look for Damien. Maris began running toward them, toddled up the hill, and bounced onto her dad's lap.

"I'm hungry, Daddy." Two dimples indented the corners of her chubby cheeks, and her eyes sparkled in the afternoon sun. Damien leaned in and kissed her forehead.

"Okay, baby. Let's go in and I'll make you lunch." He

scooped her up with one arm.

"Shells and cheese?" she pleaded.

"You got it, boss," Damien replied and called to Kate who was decorating a sand castle with seaweed curtains.

"Come on, man. You heard the lady. Grab some shells and cheese before you go grovel. Trust me, it's hungry work."

Inside the warm cottage, Damien boiled shaped pasta hip to hip with Kate who chopped a head of lettuce for salad.

"What's her name?" Jay held up the Barbie with platinum-blonde hair, scrubs, and a stethoscope around her neck.

"Sunshine," Maris answered and he suppressed a chuckle. "She's a doctor and this one's Rainbow the astronaut, 'cause girls can do anything."

"Don't you forget it, baby," Damien called from the stove, pride audible in his voice.

"Can I come check out your spaceship, Rainbow?" he said in a high-pitched voice that burned his vocal cords.

"Yes! Let's bring a picnic to Mars." Maris drew in an excited breath and ran off.

"Here you go, Jay," Kate said and held out a can of soda. Condensation chilled his palm.

"Thanks. Anything I can help with?" He popped the top and drank some down.

She shook her head and a bright, airy laugh filled the room. "Not a thing. Just enjoy your extraterrestrial picnic." Kate ruffled Maris's hair when she scampered back to the kitchen with a homemade rocket ship constructed with wooden dowels, and a plastic tub of accessories.

"Nice aircraft." He turned the rocket around in his hands and looked at Damien. The inside was wrapped in glittery unicorn wallpaper, a pink control deck, and tiny lacy curtains.

"Hey, if you're going to outer space, you'd better do it in style." Damien's cheeks reddened, but he looked pretty pleased with himself when Maris sat her dolls inside and set them on a flight path.

"Kind of puts my balloon animals to shame," he said and got up to help Kate bring bowls to the table.

"Don't get any ideas. It would take me years to build those for the kids who come to the office." Damien dumped the shells he made into a large serving bowl and placed it on the table amongst doll shoes, clothes, and various types of accessories. The spaceship got moved to the floor, and everyone sat, including the dolls with two little plates.

It soothed him to share a simple lunch with them at the kitchen table. He couldn't remember the last time he'd eaten, and the buttered pasta topped with Parmesan cheese was easy on his choppy stomach. Was Alex eating, taking care of herself? Just a week before they'd been sharing an unforgettable moment on the beach as wild horses roamed free right in front of them.

That afternoon had given him so much hope for their future. He wanted to make a home with her, whether it be at his cottage, her apartment, or somewhere completely new. He'd follow Alex anywhere. There was no one like her. Alex was strong for others even when she herself was broken, generous but forceful—even formidable when the situation demanded it.

Light pressure squeezed his forearm, and he turned to Kate who had the twinkling eyes of an old soul. "I know advice is the last thing you probably want, but I'm going to give it anyway. If you're sure Alex is it, offer her a commitment to show her you're sticking. The rest will follow." She gave him an encouraging smile before serving herself more salad. Damien and Lindsey didn't keep much of anything from Kate, not that he minded. He wasn't too stubborn to accept good advice.

"That's what Kate told me, too, when I thought I'd screwed up everything with Lindsey. It worked, clearly," Damien said to him later when they were clearing dishes.

"I love Alex," Jay sighed and put another dish on the rack. "And I trust her, and everything we have. I know we'll grow stronger together. I just don't know how to make her believe it."

"I think I could help," Kate said coming up behind them. And then she laid out the most brilliant plan Jay had ever heard.

Chapter Twenty-Two

THE SLEEK BLACK limo that pulled up at Alex's apartment exactly at six o'clock was completely unnecessary, but Lindsey had insisted. So was the shimmery black dress that clung to every curve like Saran wrap. The driver rounded the car and opened the back passenger-side door for her. She wobbled on the curb, unsure how Lindsey had talked her into wearing the strappy stilettos. She arched her body to keep her bare skin away from the cold leather seat. How had she been convinced to wear a backless dress? Alex tugged at the material. If there was any food worth eating at this thing, the art might not be the only thing getting unveiled tonight.

Breath trapped in her chest when she saw an odd arrangement of flowers sitting on a glass-topped bar. She slid to the middle of the car to take a closer look. The sea oats she recognized but not the clusters of yellow-tipped red flowers, or the branches dotted with small yellow blooms. Her pulse thumped against her wrist as she reached for her phone and typed in a search. A list of results came up on the screen, and she struggled to hold the phone steady with trembling fingers. Gaillardia, the red flowers, were likely to grow in the soft sand of North Carolina's Barrier Islands, while the yellow jessamine was the official state flower of South Carolina.

She pressed against the seat, suddenly craving the cool material against skin that was flushed with heat. Was this the reason behind the slip of a dress, the shoes, and the limo? Her stomach quivered with anxiety. Would Jay be there, too?

The limo purred to life and they began the drive to an exclusive resort in Barnstable County, as Alex did her best to stave off an impending panic attack. If he was there what was the worst thing that could happen? She could ignore him or be cordial. Jay hadn't reached out to her since their argument, so why would he suddenly want to see her? Or perhaps a limo was also picking up an unsuspecting Jay. Would Lindsey really meddle in their business that much?

Alex wound her necklace back and forth around her index finger. She was off-the-wall jittery, and barely able to sit still in the seat. If only she could be home, in her comfy PJs relaxing with Hank. Instead, he was off to a fun night with Gabe, and she was headed so completely out of her comfort zone there might not be a GPS in the world that could navigate her back to normalcy.

By the time the car came to a slow halt, Alex was sure she should've thrown a stick of deodorant in her purse. She'd sweated out every ounce of coffee she'd drank that day. Alex flung open the car door before the driver could offer her assistance and she gulped the chilly night air. Lights were turned on in every room of the grand resort, giving it a luminous glow. A few couples walked down the path that led to the front of the hotel, chattering and laughing. Alex quickly tipped the driver, grabbed her clutch bag off the seat and followed them inside. As she walked, wind caught her hair, pulling and tugging at the curls she'd styled. In the distance, waves crashed against the shore, and as she got closer to the main lobby, the delicate sound of a harp's song flowed out into the darkness. She stepped inside and pulled the sheer wrap more tightly around her shoulders.

"Excuse me," she said to the front desk attendant. "Can you point me in the direction of the Lindsey Hunter event?"

The man seemed to perk up, and he offered her a wide smile. "Certainly, take the elevator to the fifth floor. The Seaside Pavilion is the last door on the left." Alex nodded and hurried in the direction he pointed.

Usually, she couldn't stand crowded spaces, but she wedged alongside other patrons and asked the woman next to her to hit the button for floor number five. When they reached the floor and the silver doors chimed open, Alex had an urge to flee back to the safety of the limousine. She stepped out and everything seemed to slow except her flapping heart, and she held her breath as each step brought her closer to the end of the hallway. The floor was silent. There should be noise, shouldn't there? The hotel worker must have been mistaken about the location of the event.

When she reached the Seaside Pavilion Ballroom, she

briefly closed her eyes, drew in a breath, and pushed on one of the double doors. Her heels echoed off the marble floor in the cavernous room, with only a single chandelier, dripping with crystals, to catch the noise. A swell of dizziness washed over her as Jay stepped into the light from a shadowed wall. He was dressed in a black suit and a starched white shirt with no tie. God, he looked good, and wouldn't it feel even better to be in his arms? She shuffled back a few steps, and for several moments, they locked eyes, neither of them sure what to say first.

"The limo, the flowers…" Her voice was breathless. "Did you set this up? Is there even an event?" She gripped her clutch close to her chest and dared to step forward on unstable legs.

"Yes, but it doesn't start for another hour. There's a special piece that your eyes should see first." Jay strode forward and met her in the middle of the intimate space. "And you can decide if others get to view it, too." He took her left hand and placed the other on the small of her back, skin to skin. A rush of heat spiraled where he touched, straight down to her already blistered toes. He led her across the room, past brilliant Cape Cod paintings: a whitewashed lighthouse positioned on a bluff, golden sea grass that seemed to sway on the canvas, Maris chasing after a flock of seagulls. There were many, many more encircling the room, but the one they were walking toward was covered with an indigo velvet cloth. Alex splayed her fingers over her breastbone and looked up at Jay.

"Go ahead." He nodded, and released her hand. Without his reassuring grip, it was as if she were in the middle of the ocean in a cheap plastic float.

She began to lower the cover to reveal a hammered copper frame. The cloth fell to the floor in one great whoosh. Alex struggled for air as she took in the painting. Her heart galloped as she looked into the pale blue eyes of her sister who held the hand of a younger version of Alex. Tears fell from her eyes and streamed down her cheeks. She was so engrossed in the oil painting she didn't bother to wipe them away. In the picture, Stephanie held the arm of a rose-colored elephant with a gray bow around its neck. Ally the Ellie. Lindsey had captured Alex's devilish grin and tomboyish overalls—one she'd posted on social media ages ago—while Stephanie wore a dainty blue checkered dress. It was so true to life down to the cherry-red Radio Flyer wagon piled high with stuffed animals, and so personal that she was bewildered by how Lindsey had captured the lost memory. She looked at the right-hand corner of the canvas and saw her friend's telltale looping signature.

"How did you…when—" She was rarely tongue-tied but her words slurred together as she fought to form a coherent sentence.

"I called Lindsey the day after we found Luke. When you told me you had nothing to remember your sister by, I wanted to give you that. We were able to find an old news story that featured a picture of Stephanie. We took a risk on the elephant. The story said the brand was Rose Briar Collectables, but it didn't share the color or release date."

"It's the exact same one," Alex murmured. Jay gave her a few minutes to stare in awe at the painting before he spoke.

"If you want to leave it displayed tonight, you can. Or, if you'd prefer, I can help load it in the limo now." Jay stepped forward and brushed his thumb across her chin. "The decision is yours, but if you keep it up, there will be a lot of media coverage—and already one television station is interested in speaking to you about Stephanie. They said it would make a great story and help spread your message throughout the region."

"Increasing our chances of finding her," she said. "It's a long shot, but something we've never tried before." Uncontrollable tears streamed down her cheeks. "You've given me the most precious gift."

"When I told you to let the past go, I was wrong, Lex. You're the only one who can determine when or where you move on from something. I wasn't trying to control the situation, I was only trying to protect you. Right now, being with you would be plenty." Jay held his arms out, and Alex rushed forward. She melted into him as warmth glowed inside her. How she'd missed the strength and comfort she found framed inside his arms. He'd done all of this for her. The limousine and the strategically chosen flowers. The incredible painting that hung above them and the arrangements with the media. It was humbling that she meant so much to him when she'd never felt important to anyone. After her sister was taken, nowhere seemed like home, until she met Jay and found the belonging and comfort she'd always sought. In Jay, she'd found the true meaning of home.

"Wait," she said pressing her hands against his solid chest. "There's something you deserve to know. After my mother called, I was primed for a fight. I'm embarrassed to say I was also looking for a way out. I took advantage of the situation and used it to push you away, because I'm terrified of these feelings. It's not what I'm used to, and that sounds so lame, because there is no excuse for me walking out." Flutters spread through her stomach at what came next. Without voicing them, she wouldn't be able to move forward. She drew in a deep breath and stepped into her fear. "Only that I, Alexandra Macintyre, am in love for the first time with a man who fits me. A man good to the core who I can count on. Someone I can dream of having a future with—something I never dared to attempt, because before you, Jay, no one could do the impossible."

"What's that?" Jay asked as he pulled her close.

"Show me how to love myself first." She touched her forehead to his, and they swayed slowly from side to side. "I think my parents should've done better for me, despite what they were feeling. I've decided to keep the door open for them should they want to try again, but for now, I'm ready to start living my life—me, you, and Hank."

Jay reached for her hands and her skin warmed as he stroked his thumb over her fingers. She'd never get tired of the special way he was looking at her right now. His wonderstruck gaze was similar to the one that flitted over his face when the wild horses trotted on the sandy beach mere feet from them, except now his eyes swam with love and promise.

"After Becky, I didn't think I could trust another woman, but I've never doubted your loyalty. I have faith in you. I have faith in us. Wherever you go, Lex, you can count on me to be by your side—and Hank's. I've even had something else on my mind."

Alex froze in place. "I'm afraid to ask." She shivered as he trailed kisses up the column of her neck.

"Puppies," he whispered in her ear. "One or two more mastiffs."

"Two! You have no idea what an obstacle their sheer size presents." A grin split across her face—she couldn't help it. She'd never been this happy, or this free.

Suddenly, the ballroom doors burst open and their friends came through. Lindsey wore a floor-length red dress with her hair swept up away from her face, Damien had on a suit like Jay, a sprightly Kate sparkled in a tea-length gown, and Maris twirled in puffed sleeves and a gauzy skirt. Hugs and kisses were passed around their circle. Their family. She'd had one all along…she'd just had to take her place within it. After a few minutes, Alex excused herself to repair her makeup and returned to a ballroom packed with spectators. A journalist sought her out, and Jay offered his support as she shared memories of Stephanie.

"Is there something you'd like to say to your sister over the air?" A gentleman from the local news approached her with a cameraman following behind. Alex nodded as nerves flapped around in her stomach. "All right." She licked her lips and took a glass of champagne off a passing serving tray to remove the dryness that had settled in her throat.

Alex took her place in front of the oil painting. "This message is for my sister Stephanie, who was taken from our front yard in Clearwater, Florida, in 1996 Stephanie, I've never stopped hoping that you might be out there. If you are, and you see this, please come to my office building on 872 Beaumont Avenue in Boston… I've been wishing for so long."

"That was just right," Jay murmured in her ear when the film crew stepped away. "Let's go outside and get some fresh air." She took his hand and they weaved through the mob. A blast of cold air chilled her skin as they opened the French doors that led to the pavilion. Stars shimmered overhead, adding a subtle glow to the waves that danced below.

"Let's go all the way down. I'd like to walk along the water." Her teeth chattered a little. The wrap around her arms was too sheer to offer any warmth, but she wanted to feel the sand between her toes.

"Only if you'll put this on," he said placing his jacket

over her shoulders. Her skin immediately warmed, and she closed the material tightly around her.

They descended down the spiral staircase and onto a stretch of beach brightened by spotlights. She kicked off her shoes and her dress swept over the sand as they walked along beside the water.

Jay stopped and turned her to face him. The look in his eyes made her breath hitch. "Lex, there's one more thing." He took both of her hands in his and dropped to one knee. Her heart leaped into her throat as he reached into his pocket, drew out a black velvet box, and opened it. A stunning green gemstone surrounded by a halo of dazzling diamonds twinkled back at her. Her mouth fell open, and she touched her fingertips to her parted lips.

"The center stone is tourmaline, which is said to help you see with your heart. Clarity, peace, and joy are what we'll find together. I know not every day will be perfect, but with you, I'll welcome the imperfect days, too. Marry me, Lex. We make a hell of a team."

She brought her hand to her chest and fanned her fingers over her breastbone. He was asking her for the ultimate commitment. Others might think it too soon to become engaged, but for two people who rarely took emotional risks and worked so hard to overcome them, the timing was just right. She could envision their future, and it was as bright and beautiful as the ring he offered to her with an open heart. Standing in front of him with the wind whipping through her hair, she could picture them kicking back on his deck after work, walking Hank along the beach or through the city, leaning on each other and growing together.

Jay had taught her how to forgive herself and look toward a future where she deserved happiness. She looked out at the tumbling waves and let the last threads of remorse slip away with the wind.

"Yes," she nearly shouted as a smile from deep within lit her face. Jay slipped the ring on her finger, stood up, and twirled her around in a circle.

They'd set out on a road trip in search of Luke, but they'd found so much more along the way, and one quest turned into the promise of a lifetime of adventure.

Epilogue

WHEN JAY AND Alex reached the front door of their friend's seaside cottage, he gave her hand a quick squeeze. "Hey." He nuzzled the size of her cheek, ending with a kiss on the top of her head. "I'm sure Lindsey and Damien will only be gone for a few hours, and Maris is completely comfortable with us. Besides, Hank here can do most of the babysitting." The dog eagerly panted as he stood between them, his right side bumped into her leg each time he pulled in a breath or wiggled with barely constrained excitement.

When no one answered on the second knock, Alex tried the doorknob and found it locked. "Maybe we got the wrong date, but I swear Lindsey said Damien was taking her to a new restaurant... Wait a second." Alex sniffed the air, catching a tinge of burning wood. She locked eyes with Jay, and they both bolted off the steps, Hank running hard at their heels.

"Over there." Jay pointed to a stream of smoke pluming up from the side of the house. She slid in the sand and almost lost her footing as they rounded the corner, a combination of speed and distraction. Jay gripped her arm to steady her and skidded to a halt. When she glanced up, her jaw dropped.

Framing a cozy bonfire were Lindsey, Damien, and little Maris who puffed out her cheeks to inflate a colorful party blower. Flutters filled her belly, and she clung to Jay's arm. Damien's sister Kate stood with Luke supporting a colossal driftwood sign between them that read Jay and Alex are Engaged! Jay's parents, sisters, Ashley, and even Gabe huddled around the fire, and smiles stretched over their faces. She and Jay exchanged a glance, one of total surprise. Everyone rushed forward all at once to envelop them in a hug, chattering their well-wishes and congratulations. Her eyes misted with delighted tears at the outpouring of love, affection, and acceptance. Jay barked out a laugh and wrapped his arm around her shoulder.

Maris tugged on the hem of Alex's shirt. "Come see the cake!" Everyone chuckled as they followed her to a long table with filled with appetizers and sandwiches. In the center was a giant sheet cake decorated with a fondant car cruising over a map of the southern states. Jay and Alex's Road Trip Romance was scrawled on the cake board. Lindsey took out her phone and snapped a few pictures as Jay held Alex tight, a wide grin illuminating his face.

Later, they sat on blankets surrounding the fire to roast marshmallows for s'mores. A sugary, smoky scent sweetened the air as the dessert charred over an open flame. Alex snuggled in to Jay and pulled the quilt more tightly around her shoulders. It was a wonder she was cold with all the love that warmed her heart. These wonderful friends, their children, and parents had made her part of their family. Here she'd found the tender bond she'd secretly craved for so long, and it had taken the courageous man, who was holding her as if she was the most precious pearl in the sea, to give her the strength to accept the love offered to her.

"I love you, Lex," he whispered, breath tickling her ear. Goose bumps popped over her arms, and she leaned back against his chest and angled her chin to look up at him.

"Forever," she replied and sealed their words with a kiss.

The End

Footprints in the Sand

Elle Devereaux steadied her trembling hands as she reached for the frosted glass door that read Macintyre Investigating. The moment the cold metal handle touched her fingertips, she pulled them back as though she'd been singed. She wasn't a coward, but these last four months had left her stomach in tangles, and her mind rattled. Elle leaned with her back against the wall, and the breath rushed out of her lungs. The cold plaster pressed into her white blouse, a welcome relief from the unseasonably warm June day—at least that's what the peppy front desk agent told her as she walked through the lobby of the Ritz. It was always hot in Nevada.

She didn't travel nearly three thousand miles to stand in the lobby of an office building. Elle straightened her shoulders, tipped up her chin, and breezed through the doorway. The conditioned air made her all too aware of the trickle of sweat that inched down her back.

"Hello, how can I help you?" An older woman with a silver pixie cut and a lavender cardigan eyed her from the reception desk.

"I'm here to see Alexandra Macintyre, please." It took

control, but she kept her voice steady. A blur caught the corner of her eye, and she glanced up. A man was looking up at her from a manila folder, assessing her with stormy gray eyes. The intensity of his gaze made the knot in her stomach tighten, and she turned back to the receptionist.

"I'm sorry she's out of the office today." The woman offered a professional smile and began to say something else, but it was muffled by the roar in her ears. She'd spent two days in her Boston hotel working up the nerve to come to the office after being driven north by nightmares, eerie flashbacks, and a tattered pink elephant she'd found in the attic of her deceased parents' estate. Had they even been her biological parents? It was as if her whole childhood was built on a foundation of lies.

"She's planning her wedding. We're all dreadfully excited for her." Elle saw the woman's lips move and the words finally registered.

"Wedding," she mumbled, more to herself. When she'd seen the elegant redhead on the nightly news pleading with the public for information on her sister's decade-old abduction, it didn't cross her mind what type of life she led, whether she was married, had children.

"Excuse me, miss?" The man with the steel-colored eyes stood in front of her, brows knit tightly together. "Is there something else we can help you with?"

"When will she be back?" she said in a shaky, urgent breath. Her composure was slipping.

"Not until Monday." He stood straight, feet separated in an easy stance. "Who knew there was so much to a wedding?" A phone chimed, and he reached into his pocket to check the screen. "And that's my queue. Deciding between daisies and roses requires my urgent attention."

Elle stepped forward. "So, you're her fiancé then?" Thank goodness. At least she had a connection to the woman she came here to meet. He looked slightly baffled.

"No, I'm just…part of the thing." His mouth quirked into a frown, and she tilted her head to the left.

"You're a groomsman?" She fought the urge to massage her temple. A headache was brewing behind her eyes.

"Bridesman. Now, I need to go. Nancy can make you an appointment for next week."

"If you let us know the nature of your visit, maybe we could help." The receptionist stood up and came around the desk. "You look a bit lost."

"I'm not from around here." Elle paused. How much could she say? "And my visit, it is rather pressing." Honesty was always the best way, so she took a deep breath. "I have reason to believe I'm her sister." Elle's stomach plummeted as they both went slack-jawed. The silence grew to a deafening octave in the space between them. She'd never been so off-kilter. Who was she really and what would it take to discover the truth?

COMING SOON

The Cape Cod Shore Series

Book 1: *In with the Tide*

Book 2: *Caught in the Current*

Available now at your favorite online retailer!

About the Author

Contemporary Romance Author Charlee James was introduced to a life-long love of reading listening to her parents recite nightly stories to her and her older sister. Inspired by the incredible imaginations of authors like Bill Peet, Charlee could often be found crafting her own tales. As a teenager, she got her hands on a romance novel and was instantly hooked by the genre.

After graduating from Johnson & Wales University, her early career as a wedding planner gave her first-hand experience with couples who had gone the distance for love. Always fascinated by family dynamics, Charlee began writing heartwarming novels with happily-ever-afters.

Charlee is a New England native who lives with her husband, daughter, two rambunctious dogs, a cat, and numerous reptiles. When she's not spending time with her tight-knit family, she enjoys curling up with a book, practicing yoga, and collecting Boston Terrier knick-knacks.

Thank you for reading

Caught in the Current

If you enjoyed this book, you can find more from all our great authors at TulePublishing.com, or from your favorite online retailer.

Made in the USA
Middletown, DE
07 December 2018